538: Murder, Suicide and A Mother's Love

Cheryle Boyle

Cheryle Boyle
Visit my website at www.CheryleBoyle.com

Printed in the United States of America
First Printing: September 2015
Published by Sojourn Publishing, LLC

ISBN: 978-1-62747-165-7
E-book ISBN: 978-1-62747-166-4

Dedication

T his book was written for my mother, who persevered in raising eight children alone, and never for one second did she waiver on the amount of love she had for each and every one of them. Every waking moment of her life was lived for someone else's happiness. And I doubt she would have lived any differently, if she had another chance. Thank you Mom for all that you were. For a mother's love…

Table of Contents

Cast of Characters

Enter into the house at 538 Willow Way and meet the cast of characters in the lifetime of Lilly Chandler:

Lilly Chandler	Main Character
Aaron Chandler	Lilly's First Husband
Ida	Lilly's Mother
Bella	Lilly's Spoiled Youngest Sister
Milton	Lilly's Brother
Calvin Chandler	Lilly's First Son
Jack	Calvin's Last Two Children (of Six)
Laura	
Louise	Calvin's Ex-Wife
Ronnie Chandler	Lilly's Second Son
Betty	Ronnie's Third Wife
Ronnie Jr.	Ronnie's Children…
Gale	
Nick	
Maggie Chandler	Lilly's First Daughter
Donovan	Maggie's Husband
Melody	Maggie's Three Children
Jody	
Mary Ann	
Joan Chandler	Lilly's Second Daughter
Max	Joan's Husband
Colin	Joan's Only Son
Darrell	Joan's Second Husband
Nancy Chandler	Lilly's Third Daughter
Ian	Nancy's Children
Brody	
Barbara	
Agatha	
Peggy	Aaron's Neighbor/Lover
Mason	Lilly's New Lover
Milly	Mason's Wife
Alice	Lilly's Best Friend
Cass	Lilly's Best Friend's Husband
Leslie	Lilly's Second Husband
Molly	Lilly's Fourth Daughter
Jessie	Lilly's Fifth Daughter
Albert	Lilly's Third Husband
Sadie	Lilly's Sixth Daughter

Acknowledgements

Writing this book took me away from the people that I love and I want to thank them all for their understanding. Especially, I want to thank my husband for his steadfast support of me, in whatever journey I pursue. Without him, none of what I do would be possible.

I also want to thank my children, for their shoulders; the support they provided to me during this evolution was commendable. A special thanks to my son, Casey, whose creativity and collaboration was beyond my wildest dreams. He never ceases to amaze me.

My extended family's love has supported me throughout this writing and given me the determination to see it through. I love you all. Thank you for always being there.

I owe special thanks to Angela Ditch of Body Ascension, life and spiritual coach, who inspired me when I could not see the light at the end of the tunnel. Her clearings and ideas pushed me forward to surpass my self-imposed limitations.

And lastly, I want to thank Molly. Without her, I would not have pursued my dream of writing. She guided me through every episode.

Chapter One

*"Just as despair can come only from
other human beings, hope too can
Be given to one only by other human beings"*
Elie Weisel

The Accident

This house, at 538 Willow Way – within its walls many have lived, many have died, and many lives have changed. It all began at the corner of Knoll and Hammond Street. A woman moved in with five children she had birthed. Alone she would be, as her husband would soon perish. Her mother offered much help, but Lilly was alone. She worked to help the children grow, and just to make ends meet. She struggled at times just to put shoes on their feet. Little did she dream all that would befall her in the house that gave so freely? The house that watched growth and despair. The house that watched murder and mayhem. Its walls were small, but its powerful happenings were anything but. The house had a large, inviting front porch. One where you would sit with two rockers and possibly a small table in between. You could enjoy a sunrise or sunset with a freshly made glass of sweet tea. This porch itself held many a story. The house held many a hell.

It was the spring of 1943: flowers were blooming and birds were fluttering about and chirping loudly. Lilly stood on the porch, drinking in the neighborhood that had now become her home. Lilly had moved into this house because she could not afford any other. She'd had to lean on her brother, Milton, for support. Her brother owned this house. He owned all its walls and all its stories. He owned all the bad and all the good. Her brother agreed to allow her family to live there, rent free, until her husband got back on his feet. She reluctantly agreed. Little did she realize at the time what she had signed on for; little did she know that the agreement would soon be "as long as she remained husbandless." She never dreamt of the things that she would have to endure. Why, the mere thought of some of them would cause a sane person to check out, but Lilly was a fighter. She was a hard worker, she was resilient, and most of all she was loyal. She had never imagined that she would be left husbandless with five small children, but she understood that a higher power had greater things in mind for her and she felt she could shoulder all that he gave her. She often questioned whether her God knew she had petite shoulders and at times, the weight would be quite heavy; heavy indeed. Lilly always said, "God never puts on your shoulders more than you can handle." As her life would show, she would have to handle three more births, three failed marriages, two murders, four suicides, twelve miscarriages, gambling, alcoholism and incest. It would show the strength of one woman, who shouldered all of it alone, and the ongoing despair that befell her.

Eventually, seven children were going to have to grow up without a physical father; the eighth child would grow up without an emotional father. They would never know the warmth of a male shoulder to cry on. The warmth of having a daddy to talk to or to tuck them in at night. Some would remember him, but most were too young. The babies would never realize the lines in his face, or the sound of his voice, or how it felt to be bounced on his knee. The eldest would carry the last memories in his broken heart forever. The youngest would carry a scared little girl. This would affect them all, with every endeavor they would face. This was not what Lilly had wanted for her children – all of whom she loved more than life itself.

Lilly had grown up poor. She was the middle child of five, born to her mother Ida. She had lost her father to pneumonia, which left her mother to manage on her own. Lilly was still young, and this made a lasting impression. Times were tough, and everyone had to pull together to help the family out. Lilly had many aspirations for when she grew up. She wanted a loving family, a husband to help her out with the children, and as many children as God would bless her with. From the time that she was small, she dreamt of the children she would have and the loving home that she would create. She hoped to find that special man who would have all the same desires.

Lilly didn't marry young, because she was cautious. She had plans, and she worked hard to carefully carry out these plans. But marriage was always in the back of her mind. When she met Aaron Chandler, she was able to see it all come together. She and Aaron would sit for what seemed like hours, sharing all their dreams. Aaron was loving and kind too, and Lilly valued this. Their dreams matched.

When Lilly put her mind to something, she always persevered, but life would interrupt her plans – and no matter how much dedication or perseverance Lilly would bring forth, she was no match for life itself.

This dream of Lilly's, of life being joyous, with all the beautiful children that she was able to have – this is what she and Aaron both wanted. Their relationship was the envy of those around them. Lilly and Aaron had married quickly. Lilly, being pregnant at 18 and unmarried would have caused brows to raise should she not handle it properly. But this part did not offer any problems, as Lilly and Aaron were so in love, the rest was just details. With each child, their dreams played out just as they had wanted – until the day that Aaron daydreamed.

It was Saturday and he was running errands, driving to visit his parents in a nearby town. Lilly and the children had stayed at home. As Aaron sat at the traffic light, he found himself daydreaming, wanting to rush his trip so that he could get back home to his own little family. A smile gently widened his lips. The light turned green and Aaron proceeded through, slowly lifting and turning his head to the flash that caught his attention. Time stopped. A green sports car was approaching fast, running the light, but neglecting to understand what was happening. Aaron had no time to react. It was over quickly: he blacked out after watching his life pass before him, at a speed so slow that it caused confusion in his mind. Life as he knew it had just ended.

The next time that he awoke, he was in the hospital with Lilly standing over him. She was petite, with blonde hair that was glistening in the sunlight, as were the tears that had been trickling down her blushed pink cheeks. Her eyes were swollen and red. As he looked up at her, his voice caught in his throat. He hated to see Lilly cry, especially if it was something that he had caused. He didn't understand all of it. He wanted to. He tried to reach his hand up to brush away the tears, but it hurt too badly.

Lilly smiled down at him and told him that she was so happy to see him awake and that everything would be just fine. They would get through this somehow. She smiled to ease the pain that she knew he was feeling. He fell fast asleep. It was a restful sleep, because he had seen and felt her touch and he just knew that everything was okay. Lilly had a way of making everyone feel that they would be okay. She saw to it, most times at her own expense. Her perseverance, dedication, and loyalty were felt in every relationship she had. If someone had a problem, she pushed ahead to help solve it.

The doctors told Lilly they were surprised that he had made it, and that the next several days would be critical. They told her that his head injury would be intensive to manage, and she should just plan on taking things one day at a time. Changes in Aaron would be frequent and evident. She was exhausted after being at the hospital for well over seventy-two hours. She thought of her mother trying to care for five children on her own. All Lilly could do was cry. Wait and cry.

The day that Aaron was released gave Lilly hope. Hope for a new beginning. She knew that things probably would not be the same, but she did not realize how bad they would finally get. Lilly and Aaron had created their family quickly. Of the five children, Calvin, Ronnie, Maggie, Joan and Nancy, their baby, Nancy, was only six months old. There were too few times that she had felt her father's hands tuck her in at night. She had only heard a few "Goodnight, sweet dreams," whispered in her ear. She would no longer feel this sweetness from him. The memory of her father would soon fade with time, then be forgotten altogether.

As time passed and Lilly found herself caring for the children alone, she just could not manage. She enlisted the help of her mother, Ida, who would soon be living with them and helping out greatly. Lilly went to work with her sister at their restaurant, The Yellow Finch, which they jointly owned. Lilly worked long hours, and this was all that she could do to support her children. She got along well with her sister. Each one stayed at her own end of the kitchen. They would take turns yelling back and forth to one another and giggling, "Too many cooks in the kitchen spoil the broth. You stay on your side and I'll stay on mine!" The customers loved their interactions, and this only made their business better.

Aaron was a shoe cobbler by trade, and he took pride in his work. He was well known, and longtime customers would just drop by his shop to visit. They enjoyed his company and the talk that he would exchange with them about his five small children and their constant antics. Coffee was always on the burner and ready, and everyone knew this. Frequently, Lilly would stop by and leave cake or cookies for the customers. He made a good living, and he was well respected.

After coming home from the hospital, Aaron had not been feeling at all like himself. It was a day-to-day struggle just to get dressed, let alone return to his craft. He missed his customers and missed the smell of leather. On one particular morning he decided, even though he could not manage the work, that he would still open up the shop and at least enjoy the company of his customers. He felt that if he did not at least continue showing a presence, they would forget about him, and he would lose business fast. He just knew that his recovery was not going to take long at all.

Aaron decided that he would go into the shop. Lilly had baked three batches of peanut butter cookies for Aaron to take with him. She knew that this was all wishful thinking, but it made Aaron feel better, so she was happy to do it. She had sat that morning with Aaron, drinking coffee on the porch, before the sun had come up. They tried to make conversation, but mostly just sat next to one another. When the sun first lit the waking sky, Lilly noticed a glistening in Aaron's hair. She asked him to turn back and forth. It was still there. She knew; the doctors had warned her. She just dreaded what she was about to do, but she had to. She told Aaron, "Honey, just sit still. I'll be right back."

Chapter Two

*"Our hearts still ache with sadness,
And secret tears still flow,
Was it meant to lose you,
No one can ever know."*
Author Unknown

Miscarriage and Peggy

S he ran to her dresser and got the tweezers. She looked down at Aaron, who was sitting on the front steps, and a tear dropped from her cheek and landed next to him. A tear because she had to find the inner strength for what she was about to do, and for what their lives had turned into. She gently placed both her hands on his shoulders and asked him to turn slowly to the light. With the tweezers, she sat quietly and removed piece, after piece, of broken glass from his head. The doctors had told Lilly that they were unable to get it all out and that it would surface on its own eventually, and that she should just gently remove it the best that she could. This was just heartbreaking for Lilly. Aaron sat still as a mouse, with a stare from his eyes that offered only blankness inside.

Lilly returned to the house, realizing that the ashtray where she had placed the glass fragments was nearly a quarter full. She hoped that this would be the last time she would have to do this. She occupied herself folding laundry. She folded the bath towels and neatly tucked the matching washcloth inside each towel. She looked down on the bed and saw a mismatched cloth, then gathered it up trying to busy her thoughts to not take her where she did not want to go. Her attempt failed. She took the cloth, sat abruptly down on the bed and clutched it to her face where she wept deeply and fully, trying to release all that she had been through, and all that she knew she was going to have to face alone.

When Aaron got to the shop, things were still. The smell of leather and burnt coffee lingered in the air, just as it always had. But the customers never came. No one stopped by, and this caused Aaron to feel even more angry, at the accident that had changed his life. He wanted to seek out that man who had rammed him with his sports car. But that man had died instantly. Aaron was angry that he himself had not died also. He was angry that this man had maimed him so, then just left without worries. Worries that Aaron had plenty of but was unable to do anything about. How was he going to care for his family if the customers never came, and if he was unable to return to work? How would he pull and tug at the leather and stitch the soles when he could barely get his hands to button his shirt? He agonized with all these worries, that is, when he could hang on to each thought long enough to link it to a worry. When he held his children on his lap, he was so wrought with guilt at not being able to care for them that he would just tersely get up and leave the room without a sound. He also felt these same feelings toward Lilly, especially Lilly. When she would try to hug him or lean on his shoulder, or want for his feelings of warmth and care, he just gently pushed her aside and stared back at her. Frequently, he went outside to just change his thoughts and push this to the back of his mind. He could do this easily because he was unable to recall too much these days anyway. When it came to sex, he had been unable to perform since the accident, so he just avoided it altogether and made no mention of it, no discussion about it. This left Lilly not understanding what was happening to them. Lilly kept telling herself "still water runs deep," and this worried her.

Lilly woke the next morning early, just minutes before dawn. The house was quiet as everyone else slept. Lilly had been awakened by a sharp pain, a cramping pain. The cramps just kept coming and this got Lilly to thinking, worrying. She knew that she was late, but this wasn't really unusual when she had a lot of stress. Stress had explained it mildly at this point.

She lay there practically frozen in fear of what might happen next. She kept watching the clock, knowing that the children were going to get up shortly. She whispered to Aaron that she wasn't feeling well and was going to go upstairs to sleep in the spare bedroom. She said, "I'll awaken my mother to make sure that she gets up with the children." Then Lilly gently kissed him on the forehead, took a few towels with her, and went upstairs. She was thankful the girls had stayed overnight with friends. She lay upstairs in bed as the cramping continued. She knew what this was. She was pregnant, and there was a problem. She must have gotten pregnant right before the accident, because she and Aaron had not been intimate since. She felt pressure, so she went downstairs to use the restroom. With the force of God, Lilly's lifeless fetus involuntarily expelled itself from her body. She sat there, numb, unable to cry, just emotionless. She didn't understand all this. She did not understand why. No tears came that day, just blank stares. Lilly blamed herself. She never mentioned it to Aaron or to her mother. She kept this secret the rest of her life, to live only in her own personal sorrows. She was determined to not share this pain.

Lilly wanted to run and keep running. She didn't want this life that she had been given. All of this reminded her of the burn scar from her childhood. She felt that she had been cursed from that point on. Her mother, who had been making soap, had left the lye out. Lilly had reached for a toy, grabbed the lye instead, and it spilled down upon her, burning her cheek, leaving one side of her with twisted and pulled skin. She was always self-conscious of her face, her appearance, herself. Other children would make fun of her at school. Adults would scorn and scold her for reaching for things that she did not have permission to get, and tell her she was lucky she still had her eyesight and to be grateful for that. This amount of luck left little consolation. Lilly learned very early on that she did not have luck.

When Aaron was bored he would visit with their neighbor, Peggy. She was always more than willing to visit with him. Her husband, who traveled a lot, was gone much of the time. Aaron enjoyed her company because she did not remind him of anything. He didn't feel the shame with her. They would sit in her living room watching television during the day. He enjoyed watching the soap operas with her. She did not have children so she really had no worries. She made iced tea, and at times, she would add a bit of bourbon. Aaron found himself getting closer to her. They talked about having sex, but Aaron wasn't sure. He was again able to get an erection, but he still struggled. She wrote poetry to him:

> *I want to be patient, as this is what he needs, but I want to love him and these feelings exceed. I quiver inside and thoughts of him I can't hide. He is on my mind constantly, no matter what I do, is this what he is feeling too? Laws and rules have constrained us so. This I hate, I want you to know! Possibly things have transpired much too quick, the feelings have blossomed to amounts we weren't aware; however, that describes us, two people who care. But he is right – we must get beyond this and build the best around this as we can. But lest we not forget, I am a woman, and he is a man.*

Aaron found himself falling in love with her. He had never known anyone who used words so beautifully, and Peggy had the ability to touch him right to the core of his being. She also understood his pain.

He stirs within me much warmth and caring, too much to be left idle, but enough for sharing. As he toggles between right and wrong, I want to be there for him, to support the best that I can, as, to me, he is much too important a man. A challenge lies before us, creating much demand, but much worth the endeavor, for the relationship at hand. We will, together, conquer these obstacles putting us to the test, and our relationship will turn out to be one of the best!

Peggy was always excited to see Aaron. She found herself hoping that her husband would be gone out of town more. She found herself watching for Lilly to get in her car and leave for work. Ida always thought Aaron was doing repairs for Peggy and her husband. Aaron actually was repairing – repairing himself, and trying to heal himself. He loved Lilly with all his heart, but he needed clearing. He needed to clear his mind of all the turmoil from the past, all his failures and losses, and Peggy gave him just the place to do this.

One afternoon a storm had been brewing. The sky darkened quickly and the wind settled to an eerie whisper. Thunder sounded in the distance. Tiny droplets of rain started. Peggy ran to pull her clothes off the line. Aaron noticed that she was frantically hurrying, and rushed to her yard to help out. They laughed as the wind started coming up again, and the clothes whipped in the wind, trying to play keep-away. It was like a tug of war with the clothes, and Aaron and Peggy battled to get the clothespins off and the clothes down from the line. As they rushed, the wind blew harder and the rain began to pound. Their arms were both full, and when they made it into the house they both looked at one another, laughing, noticing they were both a mess.

Peggy was wearing a skirt and white blouse. Her blouse was soaked. She noticed that Aaron's eyes had dropped to her breasts. She looked down, and saw her erect nipples clearly revealed in the wetness of her blouse. Their eyes met and they inched closer. He again dropped his eyes to her breasts and cautiously reached up, touching her nipple. Peggy gasped with excitement and pleasure. He slowly began unbuttoning her blouse while looking deeply into her eyes. They both were trembling at what was about to happen, as they had fought it for so long. Aaron whispered, "Are you sure?" "Yes, I am very sure," Peggy answered. Their lips met and they slowly, cautiously kissed. They grabbed each other with abandon, and started undressing with a speed matching the stormy wind outside. The rain pounded. Their hearts pounded. Peggy dropped to the bed and looked up at Aaron. He saw in her eyes all the words that she had written, all the love that she had shown him during the weeks prior to this, and at that moment he wanted her. Nothing else mattered. He wanted all of her and everything that came with her. He wanted to run away with her and sit in grassy meadows and just hear her words. He kissed her with intent. She parted her legs and he entered her, forcing her body to jerk with excitement, with pleasure. She wanted all of him, again and again.

Chapter Three

*"In each family a story is playing itself out,
and each family's story embodies its hope and despair."*
Auguste Napier

The Letter

That night, long after Aaron had returned home, Peggy relived the excitement of their day, and with pen in hand, expressed what she was unable to at the moment – with Aaron away, and her husband just sitting across the room. She thought of how wonderful it would be to read to him tomorrow, when again they would be together.

Their lips meet, how gentle the touch. Two pieces of silk floating softly about, this would be the comparison with little doubt. He whispers quietly all his cares. He is so vocal as he shares. Small meaningful strokes with his tongue, he applies, responding to all her needs and cries. She responds in turn with movements and sighs, flooding responses in him and once again the cycle begins. This is the cycle on which they so lovingly have learned to rely. Down he moves to her awaiting neck, as he lingers in joint passion. The "Teasing Dance" as he continues his way, never being too direct, but yet causing her nipples to become quite erect. His descent, stopping at her belly, make them giggle and play as they did when small. Bringing forth a blending of man, woman, boy, girl – a special blending of all. A meeting between the children within.

The passion between them, none other have ever felt. Upon
their climax they both will melt, a special blending that will
last, and hold memories that never fade from the past. A
treasure is found each time they are together. A treasure
which will surely last through all types of weather. Never to
erode. The circle of love that surrounds, has surpassed many
leaps and bounds. The circle, the love, is to each, what is
owed. The circle continues to be held deep within the heart. A
feeling, they knew right from the start. Deep within,
Treasures of the Heart.

Lilly expressed her concern over Aaron's spending so
much time at Peggy's. Ida had filled her in. Lilly paid a little
closer attention to the interactions between Aaron and Peggy.
She had always been friends with Peggy and found herself
thinking, "Hmm, you can't judge a book by its cover."

Lilly and Aaron had words that night over Peggy, and
Aaron agreed to distance himself from her. He didn't want to
hurt Lilly and he didn't want to hurt Peggy. He felt that Lilly
was good as gold and realized that his relationship with Peggy
was only hurting him. He had enough on his plate. He did his
best to avoid Peggy for the next several days. When he did see
her again, it upset her greatly that he wanted to end their
relationship. She cried, but really, what else could she do?
They were both married and Aaron had many children,
something that Peggy truly did not want to sign on for. Peggy
shared her final poem to Aaron. They both cried, but both
understood.

Within weeks, Peggy's house was put up for sale and they planned to move. She spoke to Aaron and told him that she was pregnant. She informed Aaron that she had told her husband that it was his, but deep within her soul she knew it was Aaron's child, and she was okay with this arrangement. Aaron did not offer any options for Peggy, but she didn't expect him to either. She was just thrilled to know that she had a piece of him, deep inside her, that she could hold forever. This was satisfying enough.

Aaron struggled with his memory and healing daily, and he finally had to close up the shoe shop. People would come by and visit, but this only angered him, because he felt they did it out of pity rather than friendship. He could not accept this. Lilly was trying to hold everyone together. She would work daily to bring home enough money so that they could just eat and get by. In the evenings after the children were all bathed and in bed, she would stand and iron for customers to make additional money. Her mother cared for the children. This left Aaron with nothing to do except heal, and he was not doing this very well at all. He had too much time to think of things that he was unable to think of anymore, and this bothered him.

As time went on, these feelings inside Aaron did not seem to get better. He heard the doorbell ring. It was Cecil, the mailman. Cecil loved to visit, and Aaron rarely had the opportunity to return the politeness except on the weekends. Cecil was surprised to see Aaron answer the door and started in with his usual hellos and "Whatcha doing home, Mr. Aaron?" Aaron simply replied, "Just a bad day, Cecil, I'll have to visit with you later." Cecil, looking a bit startled, simply handed Aaron the mail for the day and tipped his hat to indicate a nod of understanding.

The stack of mail was small that day, but the return address from the top letter stood out above all the rest. United States

Government, Department of Defense. Aaron was mortified. He knew what the letter was about. The government had been calling men to active duty for the war. Aaron swallowed hard as he stared down at the envelope. The remaining mail fluttered through the air, landing scattered on the living room floor. Aaron stood, slightly trembling and full of dread. He moved to the sofa and sat down. Still clutching the letter between his fingers, he fanned it back and forth, back and forth. He decided not to open it. He didn't need to. Instead, he dropped it on the sofa cushion and shoved it aside. It lay, centered on the seat, face down, un-opened, screaming its meaning in Aaron's ear. Aaron covered his ears and winced to try and make the sound go away. He began slapping his head, again and again, to stop the sounds in his head of what he knew the letter said, "Report for Duty Immediately!"

The thought of Aaron going to war was unimaginable to him. How would he carry out his duties when he could not even be a husband or a father? He was a broken man, and to face his peers in a military setting would be his greatest fear. His head pounded with the sound of his beating heart. Aaron was unable to care for his family financially and was already relying on his brother-in-law Milton, and if he left Lilly and the children now to go to war, they would never get back on their feet.

Chapter Four

"To run away from trouble is a form of cowardice and,
while it is true that the suicide braves death,
He does it not for some noble object,
but to escape some ill".
Aristotle

First Suicide

Aaron looked over at the letter, his head pounding with the screaming that he had created within and the loud beating of his heart. He decided instead to clean his gun. If he was forced to face reporting for duty, he at least wanted to feel proud. He hoped that he still had the skill set to clean his weapon. He headed to the garage to gather what he needed.

Aaron returned to the living room and seated himself next to a tray, where he neatly placed his cloth for polishing. He opened the linseed oil and dabbed a bit on the end of the cloth. He swirled and swirled the oil upon the gunstock and rubbed until it glistened. A military shine was what he was after. He had cleaned the barrel of residue and sediment the night before. The more he rubbed, the prettier it got. This felt so good to him that he was able to do it. He thought of Peggy, and of the child he would never know. He thought of Lilly and their children and how inadequate he felt. Something caught his eye, the white envelope on the sofa next to him. He glanced over at it. Despair filled his every being. His head started pounding with the screaming from the letter again. Louder and louder it got. Tears were welling in his eyes. He looked back at the freshly polished gun. He felt the barrel, its cold metallic slickness, and slowly brushed its coolness across his lips.

Calvin, the oldest of Aaron and Lilly's children, watched his father carefully. He was eight. He was full of wonderment. He watched because he always enjoyed his father's prowess with finishing wood. Aaron had the ability to make things come alive and glisten. The wood pieces oftentimes would seem to show the essence of the tree that had borne them. Calvin wished that he could be as masterful as his father.

Aaron became silent and cried no more. He grasped the gun in his hand. He stroked it, feeling the smoothness of the freshly seasoned wood; he inched his fingertips along the impressions that reflected his initials, AMC. He traced these initials for what seemed like hours. The initials of a man he no longer knew – a man who was no longer there.

Calvin looked up quizzically as his father inserted the gun in his mouth, slowly, but directly. His father, feeling the grief and turmoil within, cried out in pain, not a physical pain, but an emotional pain. As he cried, he reached. He reached not to the depths of his soul, but further inside where he found nothing, and what he found failed to make him feel alive. Instead, he reached for the thin wooden stock, the one he began polishing so carefully the night before. It was a rich walnut. The barrel shined like no other. It was postured. It was ready and waiting.

Calvin was privy to his father's innermost feelings and his final voice, a cry so somber it sent shivers up the spine. Calvin watched his father, as he silently stood in the doorway to the living room. His father was unaware. Calvin's back leaned against the doorway trim, with flakes of chipped paint long gone, his eyes peeking around.

His father gently closed his eyes and Calvin screamed, screamed with a voice that he had never heard before. Not a cry, but a guttural sound that came from the depths of his soul. He screamed not for his father, but for himself, for what he was seeing. He screamed at the loss of his boyhood. He screamed at the loss of his own life while viewing the death of his father. "No! No! Daddy! No!" Calvin's world would never be the same. He would never be able to erase that image, never.

This is how Lilly came to be a widow. This is how five beautiful children became fatherless. The house had claimed its first. This would be the first of many. The letter, which lay unopened on the sofa, was simply a letter stating that there was "No need to report, due to your medical condition. You are released from duty."

The funeral was sad, and Lilly was bombarded by well-wishers' offerings of unwanted advice. Aaron's parents, an unstable pair to say the least, blamed Lilly and her lack of care and attention for Aaron's difficulties. They pushed her to adopt out the children, bellowing negative remarks about her inability to care for them by herself. Lilly felt numb, and as if she were just operating on autopilot. She had no clue what she had done the day before, or what she would do the next minute. The days after that, she was living in a blur. She just did what was necessary. All that she could focus on was wanting the day to be over, for all this to be over. She sat quietly and timidly, offering only a smile and a limp body for them all to hug, trying her best not to collapse instead.

Ida had wanted Lilly to give the children up for adoption when their father passed, but Lilly insisted against this. Ida knew what it was like to manage five fatherless children. Ida had experienced the same thing. Weeks after Ida's fifth child was born, she too lost her husband, to pneumonia. The family history was repeating itself. Ida was a strong woman, but her heart ached for what her daughter was now going through. She had lived that pain and did not wish it on anyone.

When Ida brought up the adoption issue with Lilly, it threw Lilly back into her childhood, far back. She likened it to a time when she was small and had gotten a doll for Christmas. The doll was beautiful, with glistening hair and rosy cheeks, and Lilly cherished it. Lilly was careful with the doll and cared for her hair so that it would not get all messy like the other dolls. Lilly's sister, Bella, had also gotten a doll that same Christmas, but Bella, who was quite spoiled being the youngest of five, hated her doll. Ida thought that possibly since Bella was so young that she would not notice the differences in the dolls. You see, Bella's doll was black.

Ida had a hard time affording any Christmas at all, and to get the children even one gift each was an extravagance. She splurged for the doll for Lilly and when it came to Bella's, she settled for the small black doll, as it was all that remained. Though a black doll, given the times, was offensive, Ida felt Bella would not recognize the difference. But to everyone's surprise, she did. Bella threw quite a tantrum when she opened the doll and saw that hers was vastly different from Lilly's. She excitedly tore the paper off the package and when she looked down at her doll and looked over at Lilly's, she threw her doll and ran off to her room crying. Ida was quite accustomed to Bella's outbursts and told the other children to carry on and ignore the tantrum. The other children did, and Lilly clutched her doll and whispered all her most precious thoughts in the doll's ear. She awoke the next day with her arm cuddling the doll. That night she had slept so peacefully.

Bella complained constantly to Ida about the doll and demanded that she wanted Lilly's doll instead. She begged and begged for Lilly's doll. Finally, Ida being tired, which most of the time she was, gave in. She asked Lilly to please give up her doll and when Lilly objected, Ida insisted. There would be no more discussion regarding the dolls. Lilly was devastated. She had taken pride in caring for her doll and vowed that very minute that when she was old enough to have her own babies, real babies, no one would ever take them from her again.

When Ida spoke those same words about Lilly's children, Lilly was furious. She looked Ida directly in the eyes, pointed her finger, and said: "No one will ever take my babies from me like you took my doll. My five beautiful children will stay with me no matter what I have to do or how hard I have to work. I will find a way. I will ask God to help me if I need it, but I will find a way. I'll rob Peter to pay Paul, if I have to." Lilly had never spoken to her mother this way before, and Ida never broached the subject again. She knew. All that she could do now was to help Lilly get through it. Ida was getting on in years, but she would do her best.

Lilly dreaded going through Aaron's things, but enough time had passed and it just had to be done. Plus, the house had very little room for anything unnecessary.

Chapter Five

"Love all, trust a few, do wrong to none."
William Shakespeare

Mason

As spring approached, Lilly felt it was time. She boxed up all his clothes and shoes, tossed all his shaving equipment and his other toiletries. She only had one thing left to go through: his private drawer in the nightstand. She never encroached on his privacy. Each of them had their own special drawer, and they both honored one another's privacy. Lilly doubted anything too awful was in that drawer, but she just had a funny feeling. She slowly opened it, with reluctance.

She placed an empty shoebox on the edge of the bed to hold his sacred items. She pulled the drawer out and placed it on the bed. There were a few car and gun magazines which she set aside to give to Aaron's brother, who shared his interests. She found several cards and little notes that she or the children had given to him. Most days he took his lunch to the shop, and she would slip a little note in there to remind him how much he was loved, and to brighten his day. These notes were all there, in date order. She stacked these neatly in the shoebox. There were a few newspaper clippings about car auctions, but that was about all that she saw in the drawer. As she lifted the clippings out, a few folded-up pages of paper fell from the stack to the floor. Lilly frowned at what they could be. She was curious. She picked the papers up and placed them on the bed, and put the clippings in the trash.

She sat back down on the bed and picked up the papers. They were the three poems that Peggy had written for Aaron. She now had a clear picture of what had happened between them and the possibility that Aaron may have fathered another child. Again, Lilly sat shaking her head. Tears welled up and Lilly put her hands over her eyes. She wanted to hide from anyone who might see her cry over this. She did not want to admit to anyone what she felt. She did not want to admit the hurt. She had been hurt deeply by a man she had loved with all her heart, and he had hurt her on such an unreachable level. She was glad that the house was empty, and that she could be all alone with her tears and her misery. For the first time she questioned her loyalty.

Lilly had been living in the past, living in the memories, and not wanting to move toward the future. She never felt she had a future other than with her children. But after finding the poems, she was so hurt that moving forward was all she could do. Move on and forget. Put him behind her as far as she could. She consoled herself with the fact that he was not in his right mind. His head injury had caused much upheaval, and he was never the same after the accident. Lilly made the decision that Aaron was gone and she needed to move on. She dried her tears, washed her face with a cold rag, took a deep breath and thought to herself: "I just need to put one foot in front of the other and put my big girl panties on and get on with it," and this is exactly what she did. She made no plans for herself, but made sure that her children were well taken care of. That is all that mattered to her.

There was a gentleman who came into the Yellow Finch frequently. He was handsome and always dressed nicely. From time to time he and Lilly would strike up a conversation, and from what she gathered, he worked in an office close by. He told Lilly that his name was Mason. Lilly was smitten with Mason right off, and she found herself looking for him every day. She would take her break, sitting at a table by the window, slowly inhaling her cigarette and finding herself daydreaming of him and wishing that he would stop by. She would blush when she saw him because all her daydreams would come flooding back to her and she felt he knew, that he could tell. They would always make idle chatter, but it was as if no one else was in the restaurant except the two of them, and that time had stopped, just for them. They grew to care for one another, and Lilly could tell that it was turning into something more. He started leaving her little notes.

As I listen, I gaze into your eyes and I see the two of us
Together we are, time stopping, life stopping, only you and me
I long for more, to hold you in my arms and dream of that day
When bliss will follow us as we reach for one another in a different way

Oh wow, Lilly thought. She felt her insides begin to flutter and goose bumps roll down her arms. She could not wait until he came into the restaurant again. It got to be that her days were just waiting for his visits and his little messages.

Lilly heard the bell on the Yellow Finch door jingle and she had trained herself to immediately look up, hoping it was Mason. And it was. She felt her heart sink into her stomach and it felt good. She became jittery and dropped all the utensils that she had been putting away. He came over to her and said, "I guess you got my note." She blushed and nodded. They made plans to go out that night, for a drive along the riverbank.

Lilly rushed home after work to get everything done that she needed to. Ida was aware of Lilly's feelings for Mason and urged her to go. Lilly bathed and put on her favorite sundress, the one with lilacs on a white background and a lilac belt. The dress had a huge collar and V-neck, which offered a tiny peek at what lay beneath. Lilly's golden blonde hair, which she had curled nicely, glistened as though it radiated from the sun. Her hair was silky, and she was proud of it.

She drove to meet Mason and could feel herself getting more excited as the miles passed. She saw him ahead on the road. Lilly could not contain herself. She opened the car window and let out a scream of joy, not that he could hear, but a release so she could better ground herself. She parked behind his car and joined him. The sun was just setting on the horizon. He had brought her a drink, Falstaff, her favorite. They drove for several miles, talking and sipping on their beer, laughing and at times crying, sharing stories of their lives and getting to know one another in a deeper way.

The river came into view, and the moonlight reflecting on the water was breathtaking. Lilly was in awe. Mason parked the car in just the perfect spot, off the road, nestled between trees.

Mason had something to tell Lilly, but he didn't know how. Feeling nervous, he read her another note that he had written. All the previous notes he had given her were just simply left on the café counter for her to find. He began:

Your hidden anxieties are easy to tell, as I, the same, encounter them as well. My uneasiness while sorting the causes and coming to a conclusion, often lingers like an unwanted delusion. The urgency of wanting much to explain, but feeling vulnerable and unsure of what I will gain.

As I see your feelings struggle with my eyes, I want to step in and stop it all; I need not feel these struggles within! I will hold you near and tell you again and again.

With my feelings I must take a dare, because should I not,
there would be nothing to share. As I share these feelings
with you as well, repeated reminding of each other, we must
tell. What a wonderful relationship of this we shall build and
reap a dome of trust within which we will dwell.

To lie in your arms, our bodies blended as one, and listen as
you share your very private concerns, warms my heart like
nothing else can, and awakens feelings of love and care, as I
feel so important that with me, you wanted to share. The
end realization is grasping how much one really does care.

Mason wanted to explain the meaning behind his feelings, but Lilly moved closer and they grasped for one another as their lips met. Lilly found just the man she had been looking for that night. She had not felt this loved since the day she met Aaron, but those days were long gone and the hurt was all that remained. She felt the warmth of Mason's love. As they lingered in the enjoyment of each other's body, Lilly smiled to herself, realizing that this was exactly what she needed. For a brief moment, she felt all the pressures of life leaving her, as they lay under a blanket in the backseat of Mason's car. He never found it within himself to explain to Lilly, possibly another time he thought.

Lilly and Mason had many a night like this. They had their favorite spots and no one bothered them. These were their blissful nights, until, upon returning home, Ida informed Lilly that the police had stopped by. They were looking for Mason. Lilly paled with concern. She tried to phone him, but there was no answer. She knew approximately where he lived, so she got back in her car, determined to find him. She needed to let him know they were looking for him, though she had no idea why. She turned the corner and spotted his car. Several police cars were also in front of his house. She parked as close as she could, and got out of her car apprehensively.

Chapter Six

"If we sow thistles, we don't really plan to get strawberries.
If we sow hate, we don't really expect to
receive an abundance of love.
We get back in kind that which we sow."
Elder Jeffrey R. Holland

Calvin's Veil of Tears

As she stood alongside her car, Mason and Lilly locked eyes. He passed her a look as if he needed her right then. She ran to him. Mason explained that his wife, Milly, had committed suicide. "Wife!" Lilly exclaimed. Lilly was devastated. She would never have gotten involved with Mason if she had known he was married. Nonetheless, this did not banish the strong sense of love that she had for him. She stood by him in his time of need; she was a good friend. Late that evening, Lilly went home and faced her empty bed, with the pillow that she had cried on for so many nights. And her tears poured again.

Mason came to the Yellow Finch as usual, four days later, wanting to apologize to Lilly. She listened, but then told Mason that their relationship could continue no more because she had been fighting guilt and it was eating her up. She felt responsible for Milly's death. She felt that she played a very real part in it and that she could not ever forgive herself. She knew that if their relationship continued, things would not go well. Mason tried to change her mind, but to no avail. He never entered the restaurant again. Lilly always thought about him and always wondered how it might have been. At times she wished that she had made a different decision, but she knew the guilt would have been too much. It still was.

Time passed and her children grew. Their cousins would come to visit, but Lilly's children never went to their homes because all the kids wanted to come to Lilly's. Everyone loved Lilly. She would help any of them out, she would listen to their troubles whether she had time or not, and she would give any of them her last dime. She fed many of them when their parents sent them out to fend for themselves. She was patient and never yelled at children – never.

One day in early July while Ida was sitting with the children, Calvin and his brother, Ronnie, were out back lighting firecrackers, scaring the girls, and laughing. Calvin always loved to scare the girls. Calvin told Ronnie, "Here, have a smoke." He convinced Ronnie that the large firecracker was a cigarette, just a different brand. Ronnie was a kind soul who trusted everyone. He believed in his older brother. But this was the first day that he found out that his older brother no longer deserved his trust. Ronnie took what he thought was a cigarette and put it in his mouth. Calvin lit it, and BANG! The smell of burning gunpowder and flesh filled the air. It was the same smell that had permeated the house the day Calvin witnessed his father's final act. Ronnie cried out in pain. His lips split open. This was the first of many times that Ronnie should not have trusted Calvin. Ida, feeling outraged, phoned Lilly to come home from work. As she so often did, Lilly felt lucky that she was able to work with her sister. If it had not been for The Yellow Finch and the flexibility she had, she did not know what she would have done.

The air was crisp as fall approached, and Lilly received a call from Maggie, her oldest daughter. She had come home from school, and to her surprise, when she went to do her chores she discovered that they were already done. The house was clean. The laundry was folded neatly in a basket. Fresh sweet tea waited in a pitcher on the table, along with a nice plate of cookies. Maggie had called out, but no one answered. She knew that Lilly was working, but Ida was always there to greet her. Ida loved to garden, so Maggie thought possibly she was on the side of the house tending to the weeds. Still no Ida.

Finally Maggie found her lying in bed. Ida appeared to be napping, and Maggie quietly tiptoed to see if she was still asleep. But Ida looked different. Her face did not look relaxed, but frozen in time. Her mouth formed a small circle as if she were singing her favorite church hymn. Her expression did not change. Ida did not appear to be breathing; not a muscle twitched. Maggie shook her, but the circle of her mouth remained. Maggie sensed something was wrong; she just knew that Ida didn't look like this. She ran to the phone and called for an ambulance. She needed to get Ida help, and quickly. Ida had suffered a heart attack in her sleep, as she lay resting after an active day of household chores. Her life was over.

Maggie shared all this with Lilly, who told Maggie, "Sit quietly and pray until the other children come home and share very little; I will speak to everyone when I get there. I am leaving right now. Just get the kids busy doing their homework and chores, just as Ida would have done." Maggie was scared, but she knew that the rest of the children depended on her too, and she had to be strong. She could do it.

It was sad for everyone, as Ida had been a strong matriarch to the family. She had guided them all to the best of her abilities. She had worked solely for Lilly and her children from the day that Lilly lost her husband, because Ida knew what it took to raise five children without a father. She knew it took a lot.

It seemed to Lilly that Calvin was always doing one thing or another for attention. He was always in trouble. From the time he was a toddler, he had always pushed the limits, and at times Lilly was just beside herself. Lilly had heard stories from his paternal grandmother that since he was born "with a caul" – also known as a veil, or veil of tears (and meaning with the amniotic sac over his face), it was considered a sign that he would either do really bad things or really good things. This happens with only one in 80,000 births. In some folklore it's a

43

sign of good luck, with such a person being destined for greatness, But other cultures see it negatively, with the person being marked by a demon, and having a soul that is already damned. Lilly always heard this in the back of her mind. With each predicament that Calvin would get into, she always feared the direction that this grandmother's prediction would go. She saw more and more that his veil was not meant for the good.

Calvin, handsome and ripped, blonde and brown eyed, was an excellent athlete and very intelligent. All the girls chased him. He failed, however, to use his assets appropriately or to his best advantage. He was drafted by a minor-league baseball team, but shortly before leaving, he was caught burglarizing a house. This ended his baseball career. Calvin would marry and have two girls. He loved to intimidate, and he would beat his wife. They finally divorced. Lilly found herself heartsick at not being able to see her first grandchildren any longer, as his wife moved away, taking the girls with her. Her heart ached for these girls. She was angered at Calvin's behavior and voiced her concerns over his lack of respect for women. This fell onto deaf ears. Calvin thought about himself and no one else. He married again and had a son and another daughter. He repeated the same behaviors, and again, he divorced.

He soon left town and traveled to Las Vegas, where he became a dealer. This was the perfect job for him, as he was slick with the cards. He could deal with finesse from the bottom of the deck. When he came back home for Thanksgiving or Christmas, he would cheat his own siblings in their "friendly" after-dinner card games. He was living the fast life in Vegas, and loved it.

He always returned home to mom, as she would stabilize him and give him food for thought. She would always shake her head, and she knew deep inside that whatever his endeavor, it would not turn out well. Each and every time, this would break her heart a little more. He soon remarried, and he was attempting to turn his life around. He became a local police officer with the political help of an expunged record. He had two more children, Laura and Jack. He again beat this wife, just as he had many times before her. They too divorced. He enjoyed tossing around those that he arrested too, and he was soon asked to leave the police force. He didn't mind; opportunities always opened up before him and he never looked back.

He took a position with the Juvenile Court as a liaison probation officer. He worked with youth and seemed to have found his spot. He was happy there. Calvin's political ties were strong and growing. Lilly felt that was because he probably had dirt on everyone; she never for one minute believed that he had turned things around or would change for the better. Nonetheless, he was appointed a deputy sheriff, and he served for a one-year term. He then ran for county commissioner, but lost. He lost more than an election: yet again, he lost his way.

Ronnie was Lilly's next-oldest son. He was married and had a son, but his drinking and gambling did not settle well with his wife, and so they divorced amicably. He remarried and had a son and a daughter, and again the drinking and gambling got the best of his marriage. They divorced, but not before Ronnie's younger sister, Nancy, helped his soon-to-be-ex-wife rack up the credit cards so that he would be left shouldering the debt in their divorce. Ronnie was a wonderful person. He would give you the shirt off his back or his last dime. Everyone loved him. He finally remarried a wonderful woman, Betty, who worshiped the ground he walked on and doted over him daily. They were a great pair; a happy couple. They brought this happiness to everyone around them. Ronnie never charged another thing to credit in his life. He paid cash for everything or he went without. He continued his gambling and his drinking, but Betty accepted it. As tragic as his illness was, neither of them let it interfere with their marriage. Ronnie took care of all Betty's needs and she stood by him through thick and thin.

Everyone met at their house one Sunday, and Betty announced what a terrible time Ronnie had had with the television the night before. She told them that he had returned home in the early morning hours; she had already been asleep. Ronnie decided to sleep on the floor. Throughout the remainder of the night he tried and tried to no avail to get a picture on the television. He turned every knob he could find. Upon awakening the next morning, he very agitatedly informed Betty that she needed to call a repairman in to get the damn thing fixed. Betty laughed. Ronnie had been sleeping in the laundry room, and it was the dryer that he was trying to tune in all night, not the television.

Ronnie was a wonderful person, which in turn made him a bit too trusting. Everyone knew this, and some would take advantage of it. His brother-in-law, Darrell, had handed Ronnie a toothpick at work. It had one end, which was very ornate, as if someone had hand-carved it just for him. Ronnie had never seen toothpicks like this before and began questioning Darrell about where he got them. Darrell told Ronnie that he had made them himself. He had a "machine." Ronnie was very intrigued and wanted to see the machine. Darrell replied, "No, it's hard to do." Ronnie pushed and wanted to know what type of wood he had used. Darrell told him that he just used pine. He told Ronnie, "If you give me a piece of pine, I'll run you a box of the picks." Ronnie gladly provided the pine and was quite excited about these new toothpicks. As time went on, Ronnie would provide the pine and Darrell would show up with a box of ornate toothpicks. Ronnie was delighted, and he told everyone he met about Darrell's Toothpick Machine. He continued to push to see how Darrell accomplished the task of creating such fine-looking toothpicks, but Darrell just brushed it off. When the day came and Darrell was held to the fence, Ronnie found out that he had actually been buying them at a restaurant chain. Ronnie was furious and so was Betty, because her Ronnie had been made a laughingstock. This did not set well with her. For quite some time, neither Ronnie nor Betty would speak to Darrell.

Maggie recalled her early years, always helping the family out. She, being the oldest girl, had to shoulder more responsibilities than the others. She didn't get to play outside much. She stood on a milk crate to reach the kitchen sink in order to do dishes, so that when Lilly came home from work, tired from being on her feet all day, she could just rest and relax. This is all that Maggie thought about. She wanted to be a good girl because she saw what her siblings were doing and she felt the pain that this caused her mother. Maggie wanted no part of this. She tried and tried to get the next-oldest daughter, Joan, to help out around the house, but Joan would have no part in it. She always had an excuse, and she was always up to mischief. Maggie found herself having to discipline Joan, five years her junior, because Ida was getting on in years, missing things and letting Joan get away with things that Lilly never would have allowed. Maggie saw and resented this. She would grow up always being Joan's caretaker.

Maggie married a military man, Donovan, who later became a mechanic. His mechanic jobs did not sustain the family financially. Maggie always had to work to help out. He later suffered a back injury and Maggie found herself always working, whether he did or not, to keep her family going. It got to the point that he stayed home and she was the one working to support the family. Maggie had three beautiful daughters. She wanted everything for them and she worked to get it.

Maggie lost her husband at an early age. He was only forty and suffered a heart attack, which left Maggie husbandless with three adolescent daughters to raise. There was no doubt that she could do it, and she did.

Joan was the second daughter born to Lilly. Joan learned Calvin's path early on, and she followed in his footsteps. She gave Lilly many sleepless nights. She often would sneak out the bedroom window and meet her friends, after everyone else in the house had gone to sleep. She finally ended up in juvenile detention. The only good thing to come out of this was that she was able to learn a trade. She attended beauty school at the girl's reform school and was able to color and cut, but she really disliked this craft and so moved on to other things.

She met her husband, Max, a military man. Max was from Kentucky, but he had been stationed close to where Joan lived. They soon married and traveled the country while he was stationed at different locations. Max was a tall, six-foot-five drink of water, while Joan was tiny and petite, just like her mother, barely five-foot-three. Joan and Max had one son, Colin. Max was very talented and could do anything with his hands. This included striking Joan. She would provoke him until she got what she felt she deserved. She would strike Max back. His size didn't matter; she was lashing out the way she had learned to do early on.

Lilly had been at her wits end with some of the kids' behaviors, so when her close friend Alice called her to go out, she thought twice, but decided to allow herself this rare enjoyment. They were meeting some friends at the local bar. And this is when she met Leslie.

Chapter Seven

"There is never a time or place for true love.
It happens accidentally in a heartbeat,
In a single flashing throbbing moment."
Sarah Dessen

Leslie and Love Again

His skin was olive and tanned, and his eyes were a vivid blue. How could you resist a man like that! A real Humphrey Bogart type. Lilly blushed when she was introduced to Leslie, and looked away in fear that he would read her thoughts. Leslie was outgoing and bubbly and made note of Lilly's bashfulness as he slid into the booth beside her. He was dressed in a flashy style, with a fedora, two-tone shoes, and a cigarette dangling. He was attractive, both in the way he looked and the way he moved. The other couple, Alice and Cass, noticed the attraction he and Lilly had for one another, just as they had anticipated. As the evening passed, Lilly and Leslie found themselves so engrossed in conversation that they did not notice that Alice and Cass had left – and they were alone.

Leslie stared at Lilly as she told him about her children and her job at The Yellow Finch. He found himself wanting to know more about her – everything about her. He desperately wanted to kiss her; he felt his mouth watering. Lilly went on explaining about their special recipe for chili, how they kept it from everyone, and how this intrigued the customers. "Why, I spend most of my day just listening to them all try to guess the ingredients!"

Leslie reached up and touched Lilly's cheek. Lilly quieted, stunned. He rubbed softly on her scar as he searched deep in her eyes. He leaned in quietly and deliberately kissed her upon her scar as if to say, "I don't care, it doesn't matter to me, I love it – just as I am learning to love you." Lilly was uncomfortable, but stirred. She squirmed because she hated her scar and hated how it always made her feel. She wanted to turn her head as she often did if she felt someone was spending too much time looking directly at it. But she didn't want to turn away from Leslie. He made her feel good. He made her feel wanted and loved, and she had not felt this way for quite some time.

She looked at him as if she wanted to speak but couldn't. Leslie wrapped his arm around Lilly's waist and pulled her closer. As their eyes locked, Leslie pushed towards Lilly and kissed her softly on the lips. Lilly wanted more, but she was torn. She had responsibilities and these were banging in her head. She couldn't look at Leslie directly. She was embarrassed. A song played on the jukebox, *"I'll Hold You In My Heart"* by Eddy Arnold, and all Lilly could think about was how perfect that song was. She loved Eddy Arnold and she was finding herself loving Leslie as well. She wanted to be back in his arms, but she would have to wait. Things were moving too fast. Leslie smiled at Lilly as if he understood and asked, "How about another beer, sweetie?" Lilly replied, "I'd love to, but morning is going to come way too fast, so I'd better call it an evening. But can I take a rain check?" "Absolutely, Leslie answered. I look forward to it."

Lilly didn't know much about Leslie, and her friends, Alice and Cass, had only known him briefly from times when they ran into him at the local bar. Lilly was worried and wanted to be cautious, but she had been long-time friends with Alice and trusted her judgment.

Lilly found herself lying in bed and wishing that she had invited Leslie to join her. She wondered what it would feel like to be in his arms, to nuzzle his neck, and to smell his cologne. She had etched in her memory the clean smell she had enjoyed while kissing Leslie. She tried so hard to fight the desire for that smell again. She fell asleep wishing and wanting.

When morning came, Lilly was awakened by the phone. It startled her from a sound sleep. "Hi Lilly, it's Alice. How did it go last night? You two were lost in each other."

Lilly responded, sounding sleepy, "It was wonderful, and it felt so good to be out of the house and enjoying myself. I just wish that it had never ended."

"Did he stay the night, Lilly?"

"I don't think so! I can't have the children waking to those sorts of goings on. I can't wait to run into him again, though."

"Well, Cass and I can arrange that. "Do you mind?"

"Of course not."

"What about Friday night, Lilly?"

"Sounds great. Let's talk later in the week and make arrangements."

This excited Lilly and got her day moving very fast. She was up and at it and just wanted nothing but to push the week ahead. Her children noticed how chipper she was. They noticed the difference in her step and in her voice. She was singing all the time and playing that same Eddy Arnold song over and over again, and dancing any chance she got. Lilly could not wait.

Lilly and Leslie enjoyed dinner and dancing with other couples. Their social life was quite active, as well as their sex life. Lilly's children were now fifteen, thirteen, twelve, eight and six years old.

Leslie loved watching the three oldest play baseball and softball. Calvin was very good and Leslie saw promise in him. He welcomed a chance to play catch in the back yard with the boys. This made Lilly smile. Leslie was around a lot by now and the children were all taking to him quite nicely.

Lilly watched out the kitchen window with wishful dreams. She had tried to put out of her mind that she was late. Again, she thought it was just the stress of trying to keep up with all the kids and their maturing. She planned on going to the doctor the next day to be sure. She refused to cause herself needless worry for nothing. She had plenty of that. Leslie was always so full of energy; she just didn't know where he found it. He always had a roll of cash as well, and Lilly and her children lacked nothing these days. This felt good for a change. Life was good again.

Lilly asked a neighbor to babysit the younger children, and the two boys had ballgames, so the house was quiet when Leslie got there. Leslie didn't live there, but he may as well have, because they were spending so much time together. He helped Lilly as much as he could with the children.

Lilly heard the screen door slam; Leslie had arrived. She swallowed hard and felt butterflies in her stomach. She asked him to sit down. Leslie was more hyper than usual this day and had a hard time sitting still. He said, "You talk, I'll just walk around and help you pick the house up." Lilly looked at Leslie and, given her quietness, he listened. "No, just please sit."

Chapter Eight

*"Oft expectations fail, and most oft there
Where most it promises; and oft it hits
Where hope is coldest, and despair most fits."*
William Shakespeare

Splish Splash

L eslie was interlocking his fingers and folding his hands, and jittering his leg. He was already a nervous wreck. Lilly was nervous too. She looked at Leslie and said, "I'm pregnant!" Leslie already had three other children with his former wife. He hadn't seen them much since the divorce. He swallowed hard and stood. He sat back down and turned to Lilly, took his hand and placed it upon her belly, and asked, "When?"

"In April. I'm already two months along!" He stood quickly and said, "Let's go do it. Let's go get married. We've been managing fine, and it will all work out.

Lilly smiled, and sighed with relief. She hadn't been sure how he would react, but this had been what she'd hoped for.

Leslie had connections, and he pushed for Calvin to be accepted by a farm team. Calvin had so much potential as a baseball player, Leslie did not want it to go to waste. He wanted him to have every chance, and he hoped Calvin would apply himself, since Leslie believed it would be no time before Calvin would be playing in the majors.

Calvin seemed to be working hard to meet the rules of the farm team. But the guys he hung out with at home were a rowdy bunch, and Calvin kept these friends even after signing. Leslie was nervous about what they were getting into. He tried to keep Calvin distracted and away from the guys, but it turned out that Calvin was the leader of the bunch. Leslie wasn't his father and Calvin made no mistake of telling him that. Lilly soon got a call that Calvin had been arrested, when he was

57

caught burglarizing the local drug store. He would have to go to prison for a short time, as well as make restitution. Calvin didn't flinch. He wasn't afraid. He was arrogant, and he knew that he would hold his own in prison.

Molly was soon born, with a head full of coal-black hair; Lilly's sixth child. She was so close in age to Nancy, the youngest of Aaron and Lilly's five children, that it was as if Lilly's little family had never stopped. Lilly dreamed that she was still with Aaron, even though she was now married to Leslie. Those days were now far away, but Lilly still found herself occasionally wandering off in thought on what it might have been like if Aaron had not had that car accident. She loved Leslie, but it was just different. Leslie was not laid back like Aaron, and often she never knew what he was going to be like. Some days he woke grouchy, and some days he would be hyper and want to get everything done right away. Sometimes he would want to stay up all night. He'd try to get Lilly to join him, telling her "We'll get everything all caught up before the children get up. Won't that feel great?" But Lilly quickly learned that she was worthless the next day.

Molly had barely learned to walk when Lilly noticed that she was late again. She and Leslie were not getting along too well because he was coming home late most evenings, and he had stopped helping out with the children. He had started isolating himself and this bothered Lilly. She frequently found pills in his pockets. He excused this by saying that his back had been bothering him, and that the pills were so that he could work. This was an okay excuse in the beginning, but after some time Lilly began to worry. She talked with Alice about her fears. Could he be addicted to these pain pills? Alice agreed to discuss it with Cass to see if there was anything he could shed light on.

Lilly went to the doctor and it was confirmed; she was pregnant again. This time was different, though; she was actually afraid to tell Leslie. She called Alice, "Alice, you've got to help me!

"What's going on, Lilly?"

"I'm pregnant again, and with the way that Leslie has been acting, I've got to figure this out. I'm very scared to tell him. I just know he is going to blow up."

"Lilly, let me talk to Cass at lunch today and see if he can find anything out."

"I'd appreciate it."

Alice called back and it was not good news. Alice asked if she could come over. Cass had asked around, with a little digging, and found out that Leslie was addicted to pills, but he was also addicted to heroin. His source said that Leslie was injecting. It killed Alice to have to be the one to tell Lilly about this. Leslie's addiction had started by using an inhaler that the doctor had prescribed to help fight depression. The inhaler was Benzedrine, an amphetamine. Leslie used it a little too much. After this he went onto pills, uppers, and more. Along with this addiction came people who had less than his best interest at heart. Leslie knew this, but at this point, he didn't care.

When Alice told Lilly about this, Lilly found herself worrying about all her children again, including the one who was growing steadily in her belly. She had to tell Leslie because she was not going to be able to hide it much longer. She was so loyal, and she found herself thinking that maybe she could just help Leslie come clean. She had encountered many obstacles before, and she felt that this one could not be any more difficult. She would try to help Leslie. She and Alice hugged and Alice told her, "Lilly, if he gives you any trouble at all, call Cass and he will come right over. Lilly hugged Alice, fighting back tears, tears that were holding her back from leaping into action.

When he got home that evening, Lilly told him that they had something to discuss. She said that after the children were in bed, she wanted his undivided attention. Lilly was very nervous because she had no idea how he was going to take all of this. Leslie was sitting at the kitchen table, legs crossed, smoking a cigarette. She sat down beside him. "Leslie, we've got problems."

"What kind of problems? I thought everything's been fine."

"Hardly fine, Leslie, if you think you need to take drugs all the time. Why don't we go see someone about this?"

"Are you nuts? I'll be damned if I will see anyone! I don't have a problem."

"Leslie!"

"End of discussion. I don't know where you get your information, but I don't have a problem."

Lilly didn't know what to do. She would manage just the way she always had, one day at a time. What other recourse did she have? She found herself back in another situation where she felt she had no choices. Lilly didn't tell Leslie that night about the new baby. She was afraid to. Lilly started watching Leslie carefully now, because obviously a lot of things had gotten by her. She was too busy with the children and life, and she guessed she had overlooked a lot.

The family had planned a picnic and all the kids were excited. They were going to "Splish Splash." Lilly loved this place. It had beautiful grounds with nice picnic tables, and the grass was always freshly cut. It was owned by the City Water Department, which maintained it very nicely and even provided a good-sized wading pool for the smaller children.

The water glistened in the bright sunlight of the day, and you could smell fresh-cut grass in the air. The whole family was going and everyone was excited. Lilly cooked feverishly that morning, making fried chicken, potato salad, baked beans and homemade hot rolls. Alice and Cass were going to join them with their children, and Alice was bringing dessert.

The children were all splashing in the pool, thoroughly enjoying themselves. No one seemed to be having fights today, and everyone was happy. Alice and Lilly had both brought picnic blankets. Leslie and Cass were playing horseshoes and enjoying a cigar. Alice asked Lilly, "So, does he seem to be doing better?" "I think so," Lilly replied, "but I'm scared that he is just hiding it from me more." "Does he know about the baby yet?" "No, I thought I might tell him today if everything goes well." "Remember, call us if you have any problem." "I will. Thanks, Alice. You have been a doll through all this."

The families laughed and giggled at the kids playing. The guys joked at how many leaners each had scored in their horseshoe game. Everybody was truly having a good time. When it came time to leave, the kids all cried, but not for long, as they were all very tired from the hot sun.

Lilly and Leslie talked about what a great time everyone had and that they really needed to do that kind of thing more often. When they got home, Lilly put all the kids to bed. She joined Leslie on the front porch. He was drinking a beer and she was sipping iced tea. She looked at Leslie and wondered when the last time was that he had used, or if he had stopped.

Chapter Nine

"Above all, we must abolish hope in the heart of man.
A calm despair, without angry convulsions,
without reproaches to Heaven,
is the essence of wisdom."
Alfred Victor Vigny

Leslie's Murder

He looked up at her and she said, "Leslie, we are going to have another baby." The air was so thick you could cut it with a knife. The silence was heavy on Lilly. She could feel it as though fifty bricks had been put on her shoulders. Leslie stood up. He did not look at Lilly but instead walked down the steps and along the sidewalk, calling back, "I'll be home late tonight." He drove away. Lilly sat paralyzed. She put her hand on her belly, as if to cradle that life within her, and said, "It's okay; we'll be fine." One tear is all that Lilly could muster at that moment. She knew she'd better save them up because there were going to be plenty more moments that would call for them.

Leslie was late that night, and many more after that. Lilly had about taken all she could. Little Jessie, the seventh child, had been born, and Lilly was tired. It was taking all that she had to care for the baby and small children. She thought back to the days when she had her mother there to help her, and she was saddened that Ida was no longer alive. Maggie, Lilly's oldest daughter, always helped out as much as she could. She was always so good with the children. The little ones always flocked to Maggie because she provided lots of fun. She was having her own difficulties, though, which made it hard.

Lilly made a tough decision. She had experienced enough with Leslie and could not tolerate his late nights any longer. She knew that he was using again, and she was becoming afraid for her children. She filed for divorce and asked Leslie to leave. He never uttered a word; just packed his clothes and left.

He stayed with his parents. Jessie was only six months old. Lilly would need the help of her older children to manage the little ones. It would become a family effort. Lilly went back to work at the restaurant. She no longer owned it with her sister, as she had sold her interest, but it didn't feel any different working there. Customers were still the same, recipes were still the same; it felt good to be there again.

Lilly was making the tenth batch of biscuits that morning. The restaurant was busy as usual. The police came in. Lilly thought it was just for breakfast, but they were there to see her. Leslie had been found in the alley behind the local bar. He had died under mysterious conditions. His body lay twisted in the dark alley the night before, with a needle hanging from his arm. The flat, relaxed look on his death face spoke of a man not feeling pain at the hands of death. They needed Lilly to come and identify the body. They had to be sure. His identity had to be documented. Lilly had a rush of adrenaline, and felt so bad that she had to leave her sister alone in the restaurant. She called on Alice to help out.

The police filled her in and said that Leslie was found with a needle in his arm, but he also had a bad gash in the back of his head. Other patrons of the bar said that he had been fighting with Clayton Ashford. Everyone knew Clayton and he would take anybody on, especially if they didn't pay up. They had been overheard arguing over drug money. Clayton said that Leslie owed him, but Leslie was not going to pay. They took it out back. After much pushing and shoving and a couple of punches, Leslie was down but didn't get back up. Someone called the police. Clayton was arrested. And two little girls became fatherless.

It was Molly's second week in school. She had just started kindergarten, but she could not go; she had to attend her father's funeral instead. She wanted to talk about this at school, but the adults told her not to because the other kids wouldn't understand. So Molly just remained quiet. Again, silencing her voice, not to be heard over the others. Jessie was just starting to walk and wanted to get into everything. She didn't want to be held; she wanted to run and play like the other children. She cried at her father's funeral, not because she knew that her father was now gone forever, but because she wanted to be free to play. This small child would never hear her father's voice or feel his strength; nor would her big sister, who sat quietly in the church pew. They grew up without the warmth of a goodnight kiss and without a warm shoulder to cry on when they had bad dreams. Daddy's knee was never available. This left them with years of bad choices in men and years of grief. One of them often searched in the bottom of a beer can; while the other persevered with the same loyalty and dedication as her mother, but to the detriment of her own self.

Maggie, the eldest daughter, found that she had always carried the burden of the family. When they were younger, with whatever difficulties her grandmother, Ida, was unable to manage, Maggie frequently found herself picking up the slack. This became a habit for Maggie. As Lilly became husbandless yet again, with Ida being long gone, Maggie stepped in once more to help Lilly.

Maggie also had many heartbreaks herself. It was as if Maggie had shouldered the difficulties and despair of all the children. She showed the same loyalty and dedication that her mother had, with the same perseverance. Maggie had three daughters, but not before experiencing many years of struggle with giving birth. Maggie had nine miscarriages before these three daughters were given to her and another in between, a total of ten. Her uterus would only hold the baby up to a certain weight, and then it would release the fetus. Thankfully, her gynecologist was a pioneer in diagnosing and managing this condition, and he finally stitched her cervix closed and delivered by C-section. Some of her miscarried babies were big enough to hold. Each time, she would cradle the baby to her chest, as fragile droplets of tears fell upon its lifeless body.

Maggie, with all her sadness and sorrows, was always the "keeper of the children" for the family. She was always there for every child. When her siblings were not getting along with their spouses, Maggie would step in, take the children, keep them out of harm and treat them as her own. It didn't matter for how long.

Though she was a strong mother figure to many, her husband was weak. With each miscarriage, he would fall to pieces, and her stepfather would have to assist her with the deliveries of her lifeless fetuses. She had to be strong; she was all she had. She had to wear big girl panties and put them on frequently. There was much family discord between Maggie and her husband: they would fight often, her husband would beat her up, and this continued throughout their marriage. She often had to cover her bruises, and often sought help from her mother. Not only did she sustain abuse at the hands of her husband, but from her brother, Calvin, as well.

While her husband Donovan was stationed in California, Maggie had taken a room from Lilly. She paid by helping out, which relieved a great burden for Lilly. One day Maggie returned home to find Calvin with a woman in her bed. Maggie was furious with him and told him so. Calvin was equally furious that Maggie would even consider disrupting his interlude. Maggie, being as strong as Lilly, did not back down and Calvin beat Maggie to the point of her miscarrying another child. This would be the first of two deaths at Calvin's hands. Maggie was always the breadwinner for her family because she was always stronger than her husband. She passed this torch to two of her three daughters.

Nancy, the youngest of Lilly's first five children, suffered greatly from the dysfunction in the home. Nancy cussed like a sailor, lied like a rug, and had no loyalty at all. She did have Lilly's perseverance and hardworking attributes, but she used them to work people and work her lies. Nancy married young and had three children, Ian, Brody and Barbara. She had a difficult time with relationships, and her marriage was fraught with violence and abuse. Nancy and her husband were quite physical and violent towards one another. Nancy described a time when she and her husband were fighting and he had tied her up and raped her; Nancy in turn threw gasoline on him and lit a match. His severe burns gave him pointed ears like Spock from "Star Trek," but not due to being another galactic being, but from being lit on fire deliberately. She always had sensational stories like these regarding relationships.

Nancy made many attempts at suicide. When relationships became too difficult to handle, she would seek attention by taking pills. Lilly found Nancy one day after she had taken sleeping pills, become groggy, and fallen. Lilly called an ambulance. Nancy's attempt failed that time, but on an unconscious level, Nancy never stopped attempting to take her own life. Something of her own doing in her everyday life was slowly leading her towards her death. Nancy divorced her husband and left him with the children. These three children had to grow up without a mother. She had no maternal feelings toward them whatsoever. This caused a lifelong rift between Maggie and Nancy, because Maggie could never understand how she could do that to her own children. Maggie kept in contact with Ian, Brody and Barbara, and she offered much solace to Barbara, who always longed for her mother. Barbara came to understand, however, as she became older. But in truth, many felt she was better off without her mother.

Nancy had remarried for a third time and birthed another daughter. She only acknowledged this daughter, Agatha, as her child. She had forgotten about the other three. She never attempted to blend the two families. Agatha grew up learning her mother's lying ways and turned out to be even more dysfunctional than her mother, as she added the trait of narcissism to all the others. As she aged, she found that life left her with no lasting relationships, and she was living in her own cleverly created misery. She was yet to fully realize this, as her biggest con game had been the one that she played with herself.

Lilly felt that Nancy had been wrong in her choices, and knew that Agatha would not become the great daughter that Nancy had anticipated.

Lilly had put Leslie behind her and was doing well with the children, or as well as could be. She had received many offers of adoption for Molly and Jessie when he had died. Again, Lilly, angered at the thought of adoption, abruptly brushed these thoughts aside. Many times she turned to Alice for help. Alice had been there through all the grief and misgivings that Lilly's life had brought her, which warmed Lilly's heart.

Alice and Cass had called to go out to dinner. They wanted to fix Lilly up with another man. She hesitated because she was doing just fine, and she really didn't want to throw anything else into the mixture. But Lilly had been lonely, emotionally lonely. She agreed, reluctantly. She wanted badly to feel the arms of a man around her again.

Chapter Ten

"The sign of great parenting is not the child's behavior.
The sign of truly great parenting is the parent's behavior."
Andy Smithson

The Third Husband

They met at Lilly's house, and Alice made dinner. Alice was a pretty good cook and it felt good for Lilly not to be the one cooking for once. She dressed in a floral sundress; it was all that she had. Albert was quiet, unlike Lilly's other two husbands. His eyes were as blue as the ocean. Lilly had thought Leslie had the bluest eyes she had ever seen, but Al's topped them all. Lilly had a thing for blue eyes. Lilly and all her children had brown eyes, except the last one, Jessie, who had been blessed with the blue eyes of her father, Leslie. Lilly delighted in them.

Al and Lilly made idle chitchat. Al talked about his four daughters and how he was no longer married, and how he missed his family. He had a soft side. He wanted to know about Lilly's children. Between the two, they had plenty of stories. Al just could not hear enough, because he missed his girls, and his ex-wife refused to let him see them often, or so he said. In truth, he never paid child support and never offered to help out; this was the actual problem that Lilly would come to find out.

Al wanted to see Lilly again. They agreed, and things were well on their way in their relationship. Before long, Lilly was again late. She wasted no time in letting Al know. They argued about terminating the pregnancy. He wanted to. Lilly wasn't sure. They married. Al voiced his desires for a boy and he was unusually emphatic about it – so much so that Lilly was concerned. He said he did not want another girl. He already had four. He said that if he had a girl, he would not acknowledge her. He would not bring her home from the hospital. Lilly and Al had many arguments, with Al never letting up about how badly he wanted a boy. Throughout the first part of the pregnancy, he still talked about terminating it. Lilly was beside herself with grief. She had felt this little body inside her, and it was way too late for that discussion.

When Sadie was born and Al found out that it was not the boy he had wanted, he refused to come to the hospital. He wanted nothing to do with that daughter. He was abandoning her just like the four before. Lilly was sick. She was so hurt she called Maggie. Maggie came to the hospital and brought them both home. Al stayed away pouting for several days, and then, with guilt getting the best of him, finally came home.

Life continued on and Al quickly came to love Sadie. He took her everywhere with him. She entertained him and she did things that just made him want to hug her and love her. He had no choice. He found it hard to resist her determination. Sadie never ceased to amaze him. This was good for Lilly. She was happy to see Al at least spending time with his daughter. She and Al fought frequently, and this made things difficult for Sadie, but Lilly felt it was better to have Al there than to have Sadie be fatherless like her other children. She had seen the damage that had caused – and she wanted better things for Sadie.

Al was not a good father to Lilly's other children. The two who were still at home bore the brunt of his rage. So Lilly tried the best that she could to bite her lip and keep the peace. Molly left home as soon as she could, and went to stay with another sister. She soon became pregnant; shortly thereafter Jessie went to live with Molly. This left just Sadie, and Al was okay with that. He had experienced enough of the other children. The older ones always brought their problems home to Lilly, which tired Lilly so much that she had no time or energy left for their relationship, and Al resented this.

As Sadie grew, Lilly and Al's relationship grew further apart. Lilly had her fill of his sneaking off, spending time with other women, and drinking. He became out of control when he drank; she supposed because of his lack of control in everything else. He rarely worked and she had to beg, borrow and steal just to make ends meet – and Al had no problem with this. It wasn't his problem. He refused to pay rent to her brother, which embarrassed Lilly a great deal.

Calvin had watched Sadie grow. She was doing great in school, and not only was everyone proud of her, she was going to be the first in their family to graduate from high school. Calvin had been working with the Juvenile Court. He had spoken to the judge about Sadie, and the judge wanted to meet her. Calvin called Sadie to ask if she would meet them. The judge offered her a job in the Juvenile Court, but she would have to quit school. She would also have to lie about her age and never mention her kinship with Calvin. Sadie, being bored with school at the time, decided to accept the offer. She was amazed that someone of the judge's standing would approach her.

Lilly was furious with Calvin about this. Lilly had high hopes for Sadie, and Calvin had just ruined them in a matter of minutes by keeping Sadie from graduating. Lilly and Al were also having a lot of problems in their marriage at the time, and this infuriated Al also. But the matter was out of their hands: it was Sadie's choice, a choice that she had every right to make. Sadie quit school and went to work in the Juvenile Court. She excelled to the point that she was soon working on cases in the courtroom, taking minutes for the judge. She dealt mostly with dependency and neglect cases, and she even managed the judge's calendar.

Sadie was rarely home, and soon Lilly filed for divorce. Al and Lilly both tried to claim Sadie, in that Al insisted Sadie would live with him and Lilly felt she should live with her.

Sadie felt torn by having to decide which parent she preferred. She was only sixteen, and she felt this was not the right thing to do. So rather than make that choice, she moved out and got her own apartment.

Chapter Eleven

*"If the structures of the human mind remain unchanged,
we will always end up re-creating the same world,
the same evils, the same dysfunction."*
Eckhart Tolle

The Second Murder

C alvin, who was approaching forty, had divorced three times, was failing at fatherhood six times, and this was not sitting well with him. He began dating another woman, Louise, whom the entire family disliked. They were not a good fit. She was pushy and did not get along with anyone. To everyone's chagrin, they married. She had two boys, one still at home and one who had just turned eighteen. Calvin wasn't happy. Everyone saw the somberness in his demeanor: a man deep in thought, too deep. Lilly knew trouble was brewing.

Lilly received a visit from Calvin one evening. He was in a mood. He was very flat in his emotions and appeared quite deep in thought. Calvin had recently lost an election for County Commissioner. He'd been sure he had cinched it, and this was devastating to his ego. He sat at Lilly's table, quietly observing, but not sharing. He hugged her deeply that night and said that he was sorry for all the years of grief that he had dropped on her doorstep. She gave a calm, reassuring hug to him and tried to stop his "nonsense talk," as she liked to call it. He walked out the front door – and he would never return again. Lilly knew his mood. She knew that he was up to something, and she was worried sick.

Lilly went to work trying to change Calvin's chosen path yet again, and called Maggie to see if she had talked to him lately. She hadn't. Lilly called Joan, and she hadn't either. She called Ronnie, then Nancy. Nancy had just seen him. He had stopped by to borrow a shotgun.

Lilly, sick with worry, asked if Nancy had loaned Calvin the gun. She replied, "Yes. Why?" Lilly wanted to smack her for being so brainless. Nancy had to know that something was wrong. She had to know that Calvin was not in his right mind. Lilly could not believe that she would loan him a gun in that mental state – or did she loan it to him on purpose?

Lilly let her other children know that Calvin had borrowed the gun, and urged them to find him because he was obviously up to no good. No one could find him. He had separated from Louise, and no one knew where he had been staying. Louise didn't know where he was either. Not yet.

The next morning Lilly received a call. The police were looking for Calvin. She told them that he had been last seen the evening before, and that he was driving a pickup truck. She gave them the necessary details: make, model, license plate. She hung up and fell into her chair. What has he done now, she asked herself? What could he possibly have done now? She felt the energy drain from her body. She knew that this could not be good. She felt sick in the pit of her stomach, and with all the intuition that a mother has, she knew it had to be bad rather than good. She had learned to expect nothing but this from Calvin.

She received a call that he had been arrested. He had been arrested for murder. He had shot his stepson whose life was just beginning, and he had also attempted to murder his ex-wife Louise. He had shot her son ten times at close range. He had shot his ex-wife in the vaginal area. She was in the hospital in critical condition, but alive.

All Lilly could think about was Calvin reliving the time he had walked in to witness his father's suicide. Did he see this again while he was shooting the stepson? Did he look into the eyes of the stepson and see himself all those years ago, all those missed opportunities and all those mess-ups with the children and with the family he had very much wanted? While he was shooting, did he just think that the bullets flying would hit that inner child and put it out of its misery? Put him out of his own misery?

Lilly grieved for her son and what he had lost, and what she knew he would have to go through from then on. She just sat and cried, probably for the hundredth time. She laid her head down on the table and just let the tears flow for a life that should never have turned out this way. A life that had started out so beautifully and ended so tragically. She cried because she knew it was not over: there was more to come.

Calvin pleaded guilty "so that the family would not be drawn through a mess." Lilly could not believe that he said this. She was furious with him. She never doubted his guilt. A mother knows these things. She knows what her children are capable of. She knows the sins that were sown before them.

Again, he was refusing to hold himself accountable for his wrongdoings. He pled guilty because he was guilty and knew it. She visited him in prison every so often just as any mother would do. She cried each and every time, not in front of Calvin, but during the car ride home. She cried for what he had had to see. She cried for his life and how tormented a soul he was. She cried for all of them, because it was not just Calvin going through these things, it was the whole family. She cried for the whole family that she had created, and how it had not turned out the way she had planned, all those years ago. She felt responsible. She always tried to look and find something that she could have done differently. She never found it.

Chapter Twelve

"As a child you made me cry, to doubt myself,
and wonder why I was so unlovable.
For years I allowed those thoughts to define me.
I'm just me. I'm worthy. I'm free.
I no longer give you the power to hurt me."
JB

Wasted Youth

L illy had known that her grandson, Joan's son Colin, was having troubles. His parents had many arguments, and physical fights, often in his presence. They would also discipline him so harshly that the punishment would continue for days. He got into trouble with drugs and stole a car, and he was faced with having to go to jail. Colin had been living with Lilly at the time, and he was upstairs, lying in bed.

Lilly was downstairs baking cookies for her grandchildren. Colin was eighteen at the time. The walls of the house closed in again. Neither the pills he took nor the pot he smoked offered him pleasure. Just as his grandfather had before him, Colin carefully positioned the pistol to his forehead and pulled the trigger. Lilly startled at the familiar sound, and ran upstairs. She lessened her stride as she topped the steps. She knew. She didn't want to know. She slowly approached the other bedroom door. There her grandson lay, as if peacefully sleeping, with a tiny hole in the center of his forehead. This tiny hole was only a masquerade for what lay on the pillow beneath him.

As Lilly stood for what seemed to be hours looking at her grandson, whom she had held on her knee as an infant, and cradled when he was sick, and tried to encourage through talks and support as an adolescent, she felt the risings of hell inside her. She felt the madness that the house had again wielded. His pillow was splotched with dark pink and splattered with red; bits of flesh speckled the wall behind him. Lilly knew there was no need for hurry. She could see. Her grandson had divided his soul throughout the room. She made the call and went back downstairs, and she waited patiently for the officers to arrive, again; again at number 538, the house that held the hell.

In her lifetime, Lilly went through decades of this type of grief. The house saw it all. It just waited, knowing that something would be showing its pretty head soon. Colin's funeral was sad and somber. A life too young to end. He had left a tape recording for each family member. He spoke of the ones he loved and the ones he loathed. It was played for all to hear. Lilly just sat patiently, as she always did. She watched all the tears that had to be shed, and all the bursts of contempt at those he had loathed, driving them from the house by the sound of his words. The days that followed were days of sadness. Lilly had to console Joan, so there was really no time to console herself. And she had no one to console her.

Lilly would always have the children over for Sunday breakfast. She always offered homemade biscuits, gravy, sausage, bacon, and the works. Never did she falter. All the families would come. Lilly's Kitchen was open for breakfast. She looked forward to this. Often she would struggle to have enough money to pay for these breakfasts, but somehow she always worked harder to come up with it. Lilly loved having everyone together. She would put together little games for the kids, and have guessing contests for the adults. Everyone had fun and everyone went home full.

Not much time had passed when Lilly received a call. It was Ronnie, and he had just left the morgue. He had to identify his son's body. They had received a call that Ronnie's son Nick had been found dead of a gunshot wound to the head. He was found by his stepbrother. Nick felt that he could no longer go on. He was unable to meet the responsibilities of having two daughters, and the pain was too much. Lilly was utterly heartsick for Ronnie. He had been such a good father, and he was questioning this now at every level.

Ronnie had three children: Ronnie Jr., by a previous marriage, and Nick and Gale. Ronnie had been married twice, and when the second marriage did not work out, he ended it with the children's mother. She wanted to get back at Ronnie, and this is when she ran up the credit cards with Ronnie's sister's help. Nancy had no problem helping out. This would be his last debt because he never owned a credit card after that. Ronnie remarried and lived out the rest of his days happily, despite his alcohol and gambling habits, with a woman who always stood up for him no matter what.

Lilly found herself thinking back over her children's lives. She grieved for Calvin and the six children he left behind. She grieved for Joan at the loss of her only son. She was now grieving for Ronnie at the loss of his son. These were grandsons who chose to follow in their grandfather's footsteps: not in his loving heart or his craftsmanship, but rather in his inability to cope. They chose to end their lives, at an unconscious level, the same way he had. This is the curse that Aaron had bestowed on the family he loved more than anything.

Males have not fared well in this house, this house of evil, this house of darkness. Lilly tried and tried to make this a house of love, but with all her efforts, she just could not battle the spirits that had already gone before. The curses that inhabited all who lived there. Lilly had lost one husband and two grandsons to suicide, whereas the women, for the most part, had all been resilient, loyal, dedicated and persevering. Lilly wondered why the males had so often been left feeling defeated and empty.

Chapter Thirteen

"The world goes whispering to its own.
This anguish pierces to the bone;
And tender friends go sighing round,
What love can ever cure this wound?
My days go on, my days go on."
Elizabeth Barrett Browning

Cancer

L illy soon became sick. She had always worked so hard, helping others to the point of her own exhaustion. She lived for others, and now she was failing. She was sitting, playing cards with her granddaughter Melody. She had a funny sensation in her cheek, then found herself unable to move the muscles in it.

Lilly had suffered a mild stroke. While she was in the hospital, her youngest daughter, Sadie, suffered a miscarriage. This new soul was not ready to withstand the depths of suffering within this family. This would be the twelfth soul that had changed its mind before coming into this family.

While in the hospital, Lilly was found to have cancer. This was the second time. She had met that demon fifteen years before, but it had been an early detection, so the outcome was good. This time, it was a blessing in disguise that she had suffered the mild stroke. She was aware of the lump. Lilly knew this all along, but chose to ignore it. She was making a choice – a choice that it was her time. It was her choice. You see, she had never had a choice in anything before, but with this she did, and she knew it. She had breast cancer. She had noticed the lump several months earlier, but said nothing to no one.

She underwent surgery and therapies. The children saw to it. They would not have listened to her not wanting treatment. They were trying to take away her choice. She patiently waited for a time when the choice would be up to God. Lilly had always trusted in God, and she had come to realize that he never would place any more on her shoulders than she could handle. She followed through with all the rounds of treatment that were requested of her. The doctors felt confident that her cancer had been cured.

Lilly's grandson Brody, Nancy's middle child, carried the burden of his mother and father's troubled relationship. He also carried the burden of the grandfather he never knew. He always tried to make peace in their family, but he was never heard. He went through life saying very little, as no one listened to him. Tall in stature, with sandy hair, Brody lay bloody and cold on the kitchen floor of the house he shared with his brother. A note lay beneath him... "Forgive me for what I do, I was simply following what I knew."

Again, Lilly had to bury one of her grandsons. Another child whom she had lovingly held in her arms, and for whom she had such aspirations. She hadn't had the opportunity to watch him grow like the others since Nancy had failed so miserably at motherhood, but she had still kept close the loving feelings in her heart from holding him as a baby and small child. All the times she played slap jack with him, and he would giggle so loudly when he won. Many times he would fall and skin his knees, and he always had to have a Band-Aid because that always would make it feel better. She could remember all those special times with him. She was finding herself becoming numb to the pain. She felt as though she had taken medicine to numb her senses. She just could not endure any more. She had asked God many times to just let her see all her children grown, and to meet her grandchildren, before taking her. This was all that she asked.

Lilly continued on with life, and one day, when she was out shopping with Sadie, she fell. This fall signaled a recurrence of the cancer. She again listened patiently to her children. She had seen two husbands die before her, one to suicide and one to murder; three grandsons to suicide – and Lilly felt that she had seen enough. She was ready to leave that house, number 538. She tried, but no one would let her go. She continued with the second round of treatments and got results from the doctor that all was clear, with orders to continue scans repeatedly to make certain.

Lilly's youngest daughter, Sadie, was not immune to this house of despair. This daughter would suffer the loss of her father just as her siblings had before her, but in a different way. Although she would live a happy life, and have it all, she would live in a quandary, with frightening thoughts of what had happened before her from the people who had come before her. She would live with their anxieties. The anxieties and fear that the house brought to others. The house would pass all of its forebodings onto others, and she would be the one to receive them.

Chapter Fourteen

"I am thankful for the difficult people in my life.
They have shown me exactly who I don't want to be."
Anonymous

Sadie's Diaries

S adie grew up with her father, unlike her siblings. But even though he was physically there, the father she initially knew had died when she was young as well – died in her heart. She would have that shoulder to lean on, temporarily anyway. But the loyalty that Lilly passed down to her didn't allow this. Sadie would be plagued with guilt for half her life. She would have it all and not realize it. She would find herself living out her mother's dreams. She would be acquiring all the things that her mother never had and always wished for materialistically, but these things did not fulfill what she most needed inside her. She wanted more. She longed for love. She had love, and much of it, but the realization that someone could love her went unnoticed.

Lilly wanted to be busy. She didn't want to have time to think of her troubles. She was cleaning closets and cleaning dressers and tossing out the things that no longer had meaning to her. She was getting things in order, when she happened upon Sadie's diaries. Lilly was somewhat surprised. She knew that Sadie loved to write, but didn't fully realize how much. She wanted to read them and understand what Sadie had left behind, and maybe she would be able to repair things between them before departing herself. She felt she was invading her daughter's privacy, but so many years had passed that it probably would not matter. Obviously Sadie had forgotten about the diaries, or didn't care that she had left them behind. Lilly saw this as an opportunity.

Lilly situated herself comfortably. Sadie had begun writing these diaries as a young adult. It was apparent to Lilly that Sadie was looking back and trying to make sense of things. Sadie wrote:

I have felt so many years of pain from splinters of this house. Just being a small innocent bystander has caused wounds that have been many years in the making. So you see there are times when the pain is inflicted and you have no control, but the control that you do have is what you do with it. Do you let it continue, or do you step aside and say "NO!" – and then choose a different path? These are the questions that I have found myself struggling with. I keep struggling with them. I want to write to let others know that they are not alone in their struggles. We all have them. We all have to endure something in this lifetime in order to heal. There will always be something to heal from. As I wander down this path I just want to make certain that I don't take others with me. Everyone has their own challenges. I am trying to connect with my inner soul and find who I am. What is my purpose in life? What is my mission? Do I have a mission? Sure, we all have missions. We all have something to accomplish. I do not think that I have lived on this earth and felt the fear and pain, without going on to share with others. Sure, my pain is minimal to a lot of people, but it is enormous to me.

When I was growing up I was always given attention; I was always given what I wanted and what I needed materially. I was not fed emotionally. I was left to depend upon the house to give me the emotional stability I needed. What I needed instead was parents to nurture me and guide me. I spent a lot of time alone and scared, and this was frightening. I would continue hour after hour, playing by myself and doing things on my own. I could go within to seek answers. I would love to be able to do that again with inner guidance. I love to go to that inner place/secret place/special place... a place that is quiet and where no one can go with me. To be alone. This is where that little girl resides. I have seen her. She has shown me many times what that place looks like. Maybe that is where I will seek her for answers.

My friends all judge me based on my family, and that's not fair. I am different. I am me! I was going to spend the night with my best friend Cindy, and we started playing with another friend, Lindsey. We decided that we would all three stay the night with Lindsey. She asked her mother, who said that Cindy could stay, but not me... Because I came from that dysfunctional family! I was crushed. That is not fair. Lindsey's mother does not even know ME!!

I want to feel that my little girl no longer needs to hide. I'm okay and I will be okay. I have many resources, ones that she has never had, and my resources will grow. I have been working on this over the years, and it is coming into my view. I will show her the way. I have talked too much about her and felt her around me. She is my comfort zone; she is my warm blanket. I see her now. I see her hide. I seek her out. She cannot be hurt by the house of hell that has bound her for so many years.

I would try to break up fights between my parents, but it never worked. Not because of my inadequacies, but because I was a child. I have lived with this *guilt of trying to fix everyone and everything, but I did not have the skill set yet of an adult. I was still a child.*

But no one listened. They always just went their way. So I would just retreat into my little world, inside my head, to that little girl. She always kept me safe and always kept me occupied. I entertained myself in my world. I would make things. I would pretend. I would create. I loved that world because it was safe. It wasn't scary. It gave me pleasure and a sense of accomplishment. Later I learned to sew. I would sit and do this by hand because Mother would not let me use a machine. I found a neighbor lady who knew how to crochet and so I sought her out to teach me. I was busy all the time. I liked being busy. It kept me from seeing what was happening, hearing what was happening, in that house.

Lilly read on and was perplexed by the revelations from a child who had shared so little. She had no idea of the pain that Sadie had endured. She wished that she had been more present in her life, and more there in the moment. She had done the best that she could, given the constraints put upon her, but Lilly felt the guilt nonetheless. Sadie had amassed quite a collection of diaries. Lilly was happy that she had peeked into the life of her child. She only wanted the best for her children, and gleaning this information would give Lilly the opportunity to understand and now be present in her final days, and to let Sadie know that her journey will be better for it. Lilly realized that the diaries were numbered, and so she began with Diary I…

I recently found out that I was not wanted, and that my father truly wanted a boy. I now know where all those feelings inside me came from. They are all valid, but I ask myself, how do I come back from them?

I'm so tiny; I only weigh about a half-ounce. I am floating freely. It is dark, and I feel so cozy in this place. I haven't been here long, only a few weeks. I can feel my fingers wiggle now. It's fun to float and wiggle. My brain is starting to think. When I hear voices, I'm creating a language for later on. This is fun. I can't wait to talk. I can't wait to meet my parents and family. I keep changing every day and I look forward to finding out new things about my body and my being. My soul is so happy.

I hear a loud voice. This voice is scaring me; the vibrations hurt. It is not a nice voice. My floating is no longer fun. I hit the side wall harder, more than once. I'm really scared. I don't understand. I feel my Mommy cry; she is very sad, she is in pain. Why am I bouncing back and forth? It hurts. I've bumped my head. I wish this would stop. The voice is saying I'm not wanted. But they haven't met me yet!

There is arguing over my existence. They think maybe I should not come to be. I want to let them know that I'm okay; I will be a good little girl. I promise. Little girls are nice, that's where the nursery rhyme comes from. Sugar and spice, everything nice, that's what little girls are made of. I don't want to be a boy: snakes and snails and puppy dog tails. Yuck, I don't think I would like snakes or snails. My head hurts. My feelings hurt, and I am just learning about feelings.

The deep voice is mad, I think. Mommy says he doesn't want a little girl, he wants a little boy. How do I change that? How do I become a little boy? He doesn't want me. He will never love me. My brain is filling with bad thoughts.

My brain is making me scared, and I cry. I didn't know what tears were until now. My brain is making me feel sad. I am worrying how to change myself so he will love me. I can fix this. I will just grow and grow and try to become a boy and if this doesn't work I will find another way. I will keep at this until he loves me. I love them, so this should be easy. I will try everything that I can think of, every day, to make him love me. I won't ask for much: I only want to be loved. That's all.

Mommy talks to me and now even she is not sure if I should be born. I feel so unwanted and unloved. Why did my soul pick these two? Is there something I need to learn? My brain is only creating negative thoughts. I don't want to be born scared and sad, but that is what I will be; that is what I already am. The synapses in my brain, all of them new, are not nice. All those wires are worry wires. I think I only have a few older ones that I first made that are good. This was before I found out that I am not loved or wanted. I will try so hard to hang onto those good wires and I will come to be loved and I will come to be wanted. I will try real hard. You'll see; I'm determined and I'm tenacious.

I know I am not wanted and I won't be loved because I overheard conversations that left lasting impressions. These were my first views of my world, so it all had to be true. These feelings of not being wanted created neurons that were the first building blocks of my soul on this birthing. I continued listening intently to develop further, but the information was not new. It was the same old story.

Chapter Fifteen

"At times the world may seem an unfriendly and sinister place,
but believe that there is much more good in it than bad.
All you have to do is look hard enough and
what might seem to be a series of unfortunate events,
may in fact be the first steps of a journey."
Lemony Snicket

Meet Sadie

I am born and I am waiting at the hospital to go home with both Mommy and Daddy. This doesn't happen because he never comes. A sister comes instead and so I feel safe because I feel like I have two mommies. They go back and forth taking care of me. She visits often, but Daddy never comes.

I cry because I am sad and I have learned when I am sad to just cry because nothing else comes to make it feel good. So I cry a lot. When I go home, I still don't get to meet him. He is staying away. I just am so sad. I want to know who my daddy is. I want to see his face and hear his voice.

Then a day comes when he visits me. I feel so safe and secure, in his arms, with all those cuddly words. He doesn't hold me long, but I'm okay with that. I know I will make him love me. The days go by and I cry a lot because I can't stop feeling sad. My uncle visits, and all the other relatives. My daddy and uncle laugh and joke about how badly he had wanted a boy. So I still know I have work ahead to make him forget this idea he has.

I grow a little, but I get sick easily. I hear so many people yell back and forth, and I still don't understand this. All this makes me jittery. I wiggle a lot because I can't lie still. I cry more because this energy has to go somewhere. My daddy visits me and looks at me. He tells me he loves me, but quietly so no one will hear him. I'm working hard to make him like me. I smile at him when he is talking to me. He puts my fingers in my mouth so I will stop crying. He keeps doing this and laughing. I like to see him laugh, so I keep sucking my fingers. I have learned to do this by myself. I like to make him laugh. I try all kinds of things to make him laugh. I blow bubbles with my slobber. I play with my toes.

I hear him talking, and he swears I have a birthmark of a shadow of a coon dog on my back. He likes to coon hunt so this makes me happy. I feel included in his life. I have found another connection to him. I think this is going to be easy. I like to make everyone laugh and smile because if they aren't doing that, then they are fighting, and this scares me and makes me cry until I can go somewhere else in my brain besides just listening to myself cry. Mommy is always busy. She doesn't like to hear me cry, but she doesn't know what to do with me. I wish I could tell her, but I don't know how.

I keep trying to make Daddy like me. He shows me off to his brother and he is amazed at how smart I am and how advanced I am. I wish I could tell him — it's so he will like me. I'm working hard to make him proud. I'm working so he forgets that he needs a boy. I will show him. I'm toddling now and learning words. I can even say adult words like "shit." Daddy laughs when I say that, so I do it again. But I'm confused because this makes Mommy mad and she tells me "no, no!" I don't like it when Mommy gets mad, but it makes me wonder why she feels one way and Daddy feels another. Who is right? Which way do I go? Which parent do I pay attention to? I think Daddy, because I am still trying to make him love me, and when I say these things he is happy. Mommy just usually leaves the room because she doesn't know what to do with me. Sometimes she carries me out of the room with her, but I cry real hard and slap at her because this is not what I want to do. She sits me down on the floor and gives me toys because she doesn't know what else to do. She tells me I am a naughty little girl, and scolds me. I stop crying and just play. When I play I can go into my brain. I have a secret place in my brain. I like to go there because I feel safe. I don't hear yelling or get into trouble there. It's a special place. The little girl can be safe there and not have to act like a boy there either. I get tired of having to act like a little boy sometimes, but I have a lot of determination. I won't give up.

I had to go to the doctor today because my bottom kept itching. I am about eighteen months old. I have a bright blue short set on and it has flowers on it. I like this outfit so it's easy to remember. The doctor wants me to take my shorts off, but I don't want to. I don't like to have my bottom checked. I start crying, but I still have to take my shorts off. Mommy talks to me, but it does no good. I cry harder and wiggle and kick, but the doctor is stronger than I am. My leg muscles hurt from being squeezed. He checks my bottom. I don't want him to look down there. Mommy always checks my bottom at night when I am sleeping. I don't mind so much when she checks me because she is my Mommy.

Dr. Benard tells Mommy something about me and I feel left out. I don't like when people talk about me and I don't understand. I go to my secret place in my brain. No one touches me there. No one talks about me there. I stop crying. I get a lollipop for not crying. That doesn't make sense to me either.

I have to take medicine, and Mommy says it's strawberry flavored like the lollipop. I have pinworms. I taste the strawberry medicine and spit it out. It's yucky. I clamp my lips closed and refuse to drink it. Mommy has Daddy hold me so that she can make me take it. I kick and scream again. I want to throw up; the taste is so bad. I wish I still had that lollipop to make the yuckiness go away.

Chapter Sixteen

"All's well that ends well."
William Shakespeare

The Perm

I fall asleep and have nice dreams. My crib is in my parents' room, just at the foot of their bed. A few months later I get sick again. Now I have a bladder infection. Dr. Benard says it came from the worms. I have to pee in a cup. I can't do this. Dr. Benard holds my legs again and makes my muscles hurt. I have to take more medicine. This happens a lot, so I don't want anyone looking at my bottom. I just want to pretend that my bottom does not belong to me. I think I will pretend it belongs to someone else. My body now has two separate parts, well actually three because I go inside my brain for secret visits, so I think that is another place.

I have blonde hair and it is so straight. No one can do anything with it. I think it is straight because I feel rigid inside and like my muscles are still stiff from the times that Dr. Benard held my legs. My Mommy doesn't like my straight hair. She wishes I had curls. She puts rollers in my hair, but I fuss. I don't like the rollers. They hurt. Then she decides to put a perm in my hair so that I won't cry because of the rollers. I'm excited to get the perm because I don't like to sleep with the rollers. She tells me that we will be doing it tomorrow. Maybe Daddy will like me better if I have curls. I'm scared.

The next day Mommy takes me to get the perm, but it is at my sister Joan's house. She knows how to do it. But she is always mean to me and I have to go to my special place a lot when we visit her. She starts to give me a perm and she has to put those rollers back in my hair and I hate those rollers. She doesn't do it like Mommy. She pulls my hair and it hurts. She does this a lot and I cry and then she pulls harder. When I tell her why I'm crying, she calls me a big baby and pulls again. She rinses my hair and gets water in my eyes and it burns. Mommy always gives me a washcloth to put over my eyes just in case. I like that. I go to my special place where no one pulls my hair. I can't wait for this to be over. No one told me that I would have to do this again and no one told me my hair would stink so badly afterwards. I don't like things that stink. I hope I never have to do this again.

It's time to get another perm because my hair is getting straighter and straighter. I know how it goes this time and I remember how badly it hurt. I cry and beg Mommy to not take me but she just ignores me. She drives there, again to Joan's. I am told I'll have to stay the night this time. I beg her, "No!" Mommy tries to get me out of the car, but I hang onto the door handle. I kick and scream and I hear Joan say what a hellcat I am – a demon. I don't like to be called names. Joan always calls me names. This hurts my feelings and makes me sad. I want to be heard and I want to get my way. I'm determined. Whatever it takes. I scratch, bite, kick, and scream, all to no avail. My Mommy drives away.

I play with my nephew Colin for a while before bed. I don't have to get the perm until tomorrow morning. I don't have to go to the special place until then unless my nephew and I fight. We are close to the same age and we have fun together most of the time. My sister Joan doesn't like us to have fun together and she tries to get us to fight. It seems like we love each other, but we fight a lot. She tells him to hit me, and she laughs. I won't take that so I hit back. My daddy says I should always hit back and never back down. We go back and forth, and if it gets to where I'm winning, Joan throws shoes or things at me to make me lose. I don't understand what's going on, but I try with all my might to win. I don't want to lose. It makes me cry and it scares me. I usually win because Colin is not as big as I am yet. Some day he will be and I will know to stop fighting with him. I have to win so that I am not afraid. I lie in bed that night, but I can't go to sleep. I don't know why. I'm trying to understand why the big people around me act the way they do. I'm so confused.

Why would Joan let us fight and then make me lose? Mommy doesn't allow us to fight. She says, "I'll have none of that." Joan always laughs. Sometimes she pinches me real hard and it hurts and I whine or cry and she tells me that I am a big baby. "That was just a love pinch, silly." Or she will hit me and call it a "love tap." I feel bad because she says it's not supposed to hurt, but it does and so I feel weak. She says I'm weak and that I fall apart all the time. She hopes I never have any big emotional problem to deal with because I will fall apart. Does this mean that there will be little pieces of me all over the floor? Will Mommy and Daddy pick up the pieces and put me back together again? I can't wait to go home again. I asked her what time Mommy is coming back for me and Joan says she doesn't know. If she doesn't know, then who does? I'm scared that Mommy won't come back for me. I was a bad girl when she left me, so maybe she for sure doesn't want me now. Then Mommy comes after all and I am so happy. I will try real hard to not get so mad next time, but I really hope there never is a next time.

I'm going to learn how to not be weak anymore. I hear a storm and I'm in my crib sleeping, but it wakes me. I sit there watching the light outside the windows. It's dark. Mommy and Daddy are sleeping. When lightning flashes I can see my mommy and daddy's bed. They are not waking up to the storm. I am getting more and more afraid. There is a loud bang. I am so scared that I crawl to the top of my crib railing, and I leap from my crib and land right in the middle of my parents. My Mommy wakes up a little and covers me up. I don't feel scared anymore, and so I go right back to sleep. I wake up the next morning and my parents say I'm a big girl now and I don't have to sleep in my crib. But I'm too afraid to sleep upstairs. I don't like the upstairs and there are not enough beds. So Mommy says I can just have my bed on the couch. My two sisters, Molly and Jessie, sleep upstairs. They are big girls. "I'm not that big yet," I tell Mommy.

I'm happy that I don't have to go upstairs.

Nancy came over to visit with her three kids, Ian, Brody and Barbara. I see them drive up. I cry because every time they come over, my toys get broken. Daddy tells me that "they" always break them. He tells me to "Run quick and hide your toys so they can't break them. It's okay not sharing." They are my toys and I don't have to let anyone else play with them. Mommy says it's not nice to hide my toys and that I should share. What should I do? I hide my toys. I have to take Daddy's side because I want him to love me.

Each night Mommy puts special sheets and blankets on the couch so it will feel like a bed and not be scratchy. Mommy always turns the dining room light off so that it doesn't shine in my eyes. She sits in the dark so I can go to sleep. The house is quiet and dark.

I look around in the early morning before anyone is up to see what my new bedroom is like. I love to hang my head upside down and pretend we live on the ceiling. I like to play "Upside-Down-World." I imagine how all the furniture would look on the ceiling and wonder why we don't live there instead of the floor.

There is a TV in my room. It has pretty dishes sitting in the cabinet. There are pictures of our family on top of the cabinet, but none of me. I ask Mommy why there aren't any pictures of me, and she takes some. I'm embarrassed to get my picture taken, so I always lift up my dress over my head to hide. Everyone laughs because you can see my panties in the picture.

Chapter Seventeen

"One of the most difficult tasks in life is removing someone from your heart."
Author Unknown

Trust is Gone

Tonight I went to bed early. I played outside all day and I was tired. Mommy and Daddy sat in the dark drinking their beer. After I slept for a while I heard a noise. Someone is walking into the living room where my bed is. It's so dark and I'm scared, I can't see. It's Daddy and he is bumping into things. This scares me more because I'm worrying that he will fall and get hurt. He stops and stands in front of the TV. I lie frozen because I don't want to make him mad. I hear piddle, piddle, piddle. It sounds just like when I go potty. I always go potty like a good girl, not in my panties. Mommy gets mad when I potty in my panties. I thought we were only supposed to go potty in the bathroom. I'm confused. This is scaring me. Daddy is going potty in the living room. Mommy is going to be so mad at him. I start to cry, but not out loud because I don't want to upset Daddy. I just cry quietly to myself. I think maybe I went to that special place to cry where no one would hear me. Daddy leaves and goes back to his bedroom. He still bumps into things.

I wait a while to make sure and then I go back to sleep. When I wake up the next morning, Mommy is cleaning the TV cabinet up. She tells me she doesn't know where the liquid came from. She just can't figure it out. I don't say anything. I don't want to get Daddy in trouble or he won't like me again.

The next night the same thing happens. I don't remember this happening when I was in my crib. I don't think I like sleeping on the couch. I don't like this bedroom. I'm scared in this bedroom. Mommy is getting madder each day. The TV cabinet has stains on it. I always look at the cabinet and wonder why Daddy thinks it's a potty.

Tonight, I stay awake. It is dark and I feel like my eyes are very, very big. I try to open them bigger like a basketball. I wonder when Daddy is going to go potty again on the TV. I cry because I'm so tired, but I'm too scared to go to sleep. What if he potties on me? I cry quietly again. I am doing this a lot. I like to cry in my special place better because no one tells me I'm weak. Crying feels good.

I hear footsteps. Daddy falls down and he says that S-word again. He stands up and starts going potty, just like all the other nights. Mommy is awake too, and yells at him, and he gets real mad. He goes to the bathroom to potty this time, just like where I go. Mommy starts cleaning it up and all the while she is saying bad things about Daddy and she says he is always in a drunken stupor. What does that mean? What is a drunken stupor? I guess when you have one of those you can't help what you do. Mommy should be more understanding if Daddy can't help it. I cry because I feel bad for Daddy and I feel bad that Mommy is mad at him. It seems like everyone is always mad at Daddy and I always hear them talk about how much they don't like him and that he is mean. They are wrong. Daddy is nice. He is always nice to me. He talks to me all the time, but he yells at me too. He wants me to do things better, that's why he yells. I will try harder. I guess if I were a boy I would do things better and he would not have to yell.

I want a horse. I tell Daddy this when we are building a box in the garage. I like to build things with Daddy because these are things that boys do and I am able to show him that I can do this too. He seems happy with me helping. "What would you do with a horse?" he asks.

"I would ride it. I would ride fast."

"Where would you keep it?"

"In our yard."

"We can't, it's against the law."

"But I want one," I begged. I'm good at begging. Daddy says I drive him crazy with my begging.

The next day Daddy took me to a sale and we bought a horse. I was so happy. I named her Victoria, just like the Queen, but I want to call her Vicky. She has spots just like the horse on Bonanza. I watch "Bonanza" all the time with Daddy, and "Gunsmoke." I have to be real quiet then, but I don't mind. I guess if Daddy bought me a horse, then he must like me.

At bedtime, I hear Mommy talking about another storm. I am scared when it storms and it is so loud, I have a hard time going to my special place. Mommy tucks me in and the blankets are all warm up to my neck. I fall right asleep. I am awakened by the crash of thunder again and I'm scared. I run and get in Mommy and Daddy's bed right in between them just like I used to jump from my crib. I fall right to sleep.

It's early morning and Mommy gets up to make breakfast. I slide over to her side because it's warm. I fall fast asleep. I wake up because something doesn't feel right. Daddy has moved close to me. Oh, maybe we are going to snuggle. Daddy smells. It's a beer smell. I don't like that smell. I am lying on my side, but I can smell his stinky breath over my shoulder. His hand touches my belly. This is different. He puts his hand in my panties and I freeze. It's just like when the doctor checked my bottom. I cannot move. My body is so stiff. I'm paralyzed. I want to get up and run, but I am frozen in place. He touches me where no one is supposed to. I want to cry. I can't even cry in my special place because I am so afraid. I don't like that part of my body anymore. Only bad things happen down there. The scared little girl says "NO Daddy Don't!" but her voice won't come out of my throat cause my throat is frozen. I finally say it, and loud, and Daddy stops. I jump out of the warm bed that froze me, and Daddy says, "I'm sorry, I thought you were Mommy."

I run to the kitchen where Mommy is and I hug her close. She says, "Well, good morning to you too." I don't say anything because I don't want Daddy to be mad at me and I don't want Daddy to get into trouble. Mommy makes me breakfast. Daddy joins us. He doesn't say anything either. Life continues as usual, except for two things:

1) I don't feel close to my daddy anymore. He died that day, that moment. I still want him to love me, but he doesn't have to hug me or touch me. I don't want anybody to touch me. I have now learned what

body space is. I will keep him and everyone else "this far away" so that never happens again.

2) My body has definitely split in two. My top half is the working half and the bottom half is only there; it serves no purpose other than to potty from. We no longer talk to that part because it causes us pain. We are making no brain connections to that part.

The pain is in our head. Daddy scared the little girl too badly. She will guard that area and keep vigilant watch over it. This is her house of pain. Now, every moment, she must be on guard and not let anyone close. She is the "Keeper of the Gates." I am so sad that I lost my daddy that day. He was very special to me and I loved to snuggle with him and feel close. I love him so much, but I can't trust him. I now have to be careful around him. Just like I can't trust my sister Joan anymore to not hurt me in some way. There are just some people you have to watch out for and keep your distance from. My little girl is now watching everyone and looking to see what all their actions mean, and making judgments from those actions.

Chapter Eighteen

*"I think it's odd that grownups quarrel so easily and
so often and about such petty matters.
Up to now I always thought bickering was just something
children did and that they outgrew it."*
Anne Frank

The Arrest

I was always afraid of the upstairs; this is why I sleep on the couch downstairs. My two sisters sleep upstairs. I never went up there except to help Mommy clean their rooms.

Mommy and Daddy are fighting again. I beg Mommy to just be quiet. "Please be quiet. If you don't talk, then he has no one to fight with. He will stop talking. Please stop!" I am so scared. I wish I could make them stop this. I will try and just keep trying because I am determined. I wish that they liked each other. I think that they do most of the time. It seems that these things always happen at night. At night is when I worry more. I try to play during the day and not think about things. I think more thoughts like "How can I stop them the next time that they fight? What causes these fights? What can I do to make them happy?" I will be a good little girl. I try hard to be a good little girl. I want them to like me, and maybe they fight because I am here now and they didn't want me. I should not have come to these parents, but I know that I can make them love me. I still want to be loved. I will just try harder.

The yelling keeps going in between the beer again. I watch quietly while pretending to be asleep on the couch. Daddy pushes Mommy on the shoulder sometimes. This really scares me because Mommy looks like it hurts her. I don't want Daddy to hurt Mommy. I cry so that maybe they will stop. I cry real loud and Mommy stops fighting with Daddy and comes over to me. "Go back to sleep, little one," she says.

I can't go back to sleep if you keep fighting. I'm scared! You just be quiet and he'll stop. Mommy just looked at me and said, "Sadie, just close your eyes."

I try really hard to close my eyes, but I want to see if they stop. I lie there, frozen again, because the little girl inside me is scared and she's hiding in her secret place again. She hates the loud yelling. I put my hands over my ears, but I can still hear. Daddy stands up and he is close to Mommy, pointing his finger in her face. Mommy always told me never to point. Now I know why it is bad to point. Pointing makes people mean. Mommy smacks Daddy's hand away and now she stands up. They are pushing each other. I am getting more scared because I know that someone is going to get hurt. Mommy looks scared, too.

Mommy runs out the front door. I don't know where she went, but she forgot to take me with her. Only Daddy is here with me, and he is talking to himself and stomping his foot. I can't go upstairs to get my sisters because they are spending the night somewhere else. I'm too scared to go upstairs anyway. I'll just lie here frozen. Frozen is better. I'll make myself real little and go to my secret place. I feel better there. I cover my head up with the blanket. If I'm in my secret place, then Daddy will think I am asleep and he won't bother me. Daddy sits back down at the table. He keeps drinking his beer. Why doesn't he go look for Mommy? Mommy is by herself in the dark outside. I'm really scared for her.

Someone knocks on the door. Daddy doesn't move. He doesn't answer it. There is another knock that is real loud, and it scares me from my secret place. Daddy starts talking to himself again and gets up to answer the door. The man pushes his way in. I'm sitting up on the couch now. The knocking made me jump up.

I have my favorite pajamas on. They are all pastel and real silky feeling. I love to feel silk. Lots of times when I suck my fingers I will rub something silky. That makes me go to sleep very fast. I can't go to sleep now. The pajamas have ruffles and each ruffle has a different color: light pink, light yellow, light aqua. Aqua is my favorite color. They call these pajamas "baby dolls." I don't know why, because they aren't for baby dolls. My baby dolls don't have pajamas that are silky; they only have ones that Mommy has sewed for me.

The man is talking to Daddy and then Mommy comes back home. She talks to the man also. Daddy is getting madder and tries to push Mommy in front of the man. The man grabs Daddy and spins him around. Another man is helping him. They have big guns. I'm afraid of guns too. Daddy always has guns and cleans them. I get real scared when he cleans the guns. I'm afraid that he will make a mistake and it will shoot. The two men put these things on Daddy's hands and he can't move. I am so scared. Are they going to do that to me next, I wonder? I get up off the couch.

I can talk to them and make them understand that this is my daddy and that I need my daddy. They are getting ready to take my daddy somewhere. They say he is under arrested, that's how I say it. I know what this means and I won't let them take him. I go over to one of the men and pull on his pant leg and try to reach his arm and pull it away so that he can't have a hold of my daddy. "You can't take my daddy. Leave my daddy alone! You are hurting my daddy." I hit the man because I think that he is mean. I am so afraid, but I have to try. I am determined. I will help my daddy.

The man picks me up real fast. I am hitting at his face and I am real scared because Mommy is telling me to stop. "He is a police officer and he is going to help us." I always thought police officers helped us, but he is taking my daddy away. I hit and hit at him and he holds my hands down. I scream and kick and I try to bite him. I don't know what else to do. I have to try everything that I can, just like when I have to go to my sister's to get a permanent and I don't want my hair pulled.

The man tells me, "Young lady, you should be in bed! What are you doing up at this hour?" He is walking with me now. Where is he taking me? I am so scared and I am shaking. But I still am trying to hit him. I don't like him. He is taking me upstairs. I don't want to go upstairs. I'm afraid. I bite my lip and it is bleeding. I scream and kick some more. "I don't want to go upstairs. I never go upstairs." He takes me to the second bedroom; it is all dark and I don't know where I am or what is up here. I don't feel safe and I am so scared. I try to go to my little place, but I am too scared to even do that. He lays me down on the bed and puts covers on me. I kick them off and try to get up. I can run fast. I'll try to get away from him.

He holds me down and I am frozen again. My leg muscles hurt just like in the doctor's office. I stop fighting. He covers me again and tells me I need to stay there and get myself to sleep. "You should be sleeping, young lady. Now go to sleep. Do not get up!" I am scared that he might put me under arrested. He leaves the room. I am still frozen. The little girl inside my head is talking real fast and I start crying. I cry real hard and it makes it hard for me to breathe. I keep losing my breath. Maybe I will just lose my breath and lie here and die. Mommy will not know where I am and no one will know that I died. I am too scared to think. That closet is over there in the dark room. The little girl thinks that maybe something in the closet is going to come out and get me. I want to go downstairs, but I'm too frozen to move. My legs won't move. I can't walk down there. And what if that man is still here? I cry some more and I scream and scream, but not loud, in my head. No one can hear my screams. I fall asleep.

I wake in the morning because Mommy is shaking me. "Get up, honey," she says. "Time for breakfast." I sit up and I look around. I had never seen this room before. I see the creepy closet across the room. I ask Mommy, "Can we go downstairs now?" She smiles and says yes. I jump out of the bed and run as fast as I can. The ruffles from my silky jamas are bouncing like a bouncy dress. I love these jamas. Mommy says I sure must be hungry to run that fast downstairs. No, Mommy, I'm not hungry, I'm scared. But I don't say anything because it wouldn't matter; I just talk to that little girl again. She always listens. She tells me what I should do. She looks out for me.

I go downstairs and eat my breakfast, but Daddy isn't there. Mommy says that Daddy is busy today. I go outside and talk to myself and play all day making mud pies. I like to make mud pies; that's what Mommy calls them. I call them cookies. I am making cookies for all the neighbor kids and my sisters. I make sure that I mix the mud just right. Mommy gave me a bowl and a spoon. She gave me some newspapers to dry them on. I carefully make each spoonful round and just right because I want my cookies to be just perfect for everyone. I put them on the newspapers because this is my oven and that's how I bake the cookies. I have fun making cookies.

Mommy calls me in for lunch. After lunch, she washes my face. She talks on the phone a lot today. I don't listen because I am busy with my doll babies. I tell them about all the cookies I made and that we will have them for our snack later today. Mommy tells me it is naptime. I'm tired today, so I don't argue; I just fall asleep fast. When I wake up, Mommy says it's time for a snack, but I don't want a snack, I just want to run outside and see how my cookies turned out. My cookies are perfect. They are all baked hard from the sun and I run back in to tell Mommy. I have an orange that Mommy has cut for me and put on the plate like a flower. I love flowers. She sprinkled my orange with powdered sugar. I like this. I hurry and eat my orange. I get my baby dolls and we go back outside. I sit my dolls in the chairs outside and pretend they are my friends. I like these friends because they talk a lot to that little girl in my head and she is happy when the dolls are talking to her.

I go on car rides with my family. It's what we do on a Sunday afternoon for fun. My daddy takes us to scary places where they have bridges with only two boards. He has to keep the tires on the two boards. I just worry he will miss. We are in the country and there are no houses around. I'm scared that if something happens there will be no one to save us. Mommy and Daddy are in the front seat. They are talking and sometimes it's loud. I tell Mommy I want to go back home. I don't like riding in the car: my tummy hurts. Daddy says, "Look the scary bridge!" I start crying and he laughs. Mommy gets after him, but he still laughs.

I still cry, but I just do it in my head where no one can hear me because no one cares anyway. I get down on the floorboards of the car because that is where I want to be when we hit the water. I curl up in a ball because I want to be as tiny as I can right now. I think inside my head that if I stay there, water won't get me, and I won't have to fall because I am already low in the car. I no longer cry inside, just whimper. I whimper in a rhythm like making a song and this always puts me to sleep. I suck on my fingers because that makes me feel better too. I fall fast asleep, curled up, tiny and small.

When I wake up we are already back home and I am so glad. I don't want to do that again, but every Sunday that's what we do. I hate the car and I hate those bridges, scary bridges. I don't like when Daddy laughs and thinks he's funny, but no one else does.

My sister is funny. She has friends over and they like to do silly things. One night they wanted pizza and it was late. I had already been sleeping, but yelling woke me up. Daddy was mad that they wanted to eat so late. He didn't want them to make pizza. He and Mommy were yelling at each other. He went to the basement and turned the gas off to the house so the stove would not cook. Mommy was so mad. They were pushing each other and yelling. My daddy had a gun and by pulling it out maybe he thought he might win the argument. He didn't know what else to do.

Chapter Nineteen

"Anxiety is the handmaiden of creativity"
T.S. Eliot

Willard

*H*e always did this. When the argument got beyond him, he just got his gun for help. Mommy called the police. They knew our address. I cried and cried because I was so scared. I tried to get them to stop arguing. I always tried to fix them. My sister and her friend had to go to bed without pizza. I finally fell back sleep worrying if Daddy was going to come to the living room falling down again.

I had a dream that night about being in a car, driving, and we were even with the water. A big bunch of water that you can see forever. We have to keep the car on a narrow road or we will go into the water. I don't want to drown. We start to go into the water and we all get out of the car and try to swim, but my legs and arms are so tired. I keep trying because I am determined. I wake up and Mommy is making breakfast and it smells good. I have this dream all the time, the same one. I don't like water anymore, or cars, or people that hurt you. I wish I would stop having this dream.

I am getting older now and I go places with Daddy a lot. Daddy always has someplace to go because he doesn't go to work anymore. Mommy and Daddy fight about this. They are still fighting all the time, almost every night, but I don't listen anymore. I just talk to my dolls or the little girl. I still get scared, but I'm older now and I think that I have gotten used to it. I don't try to fix them anymore.

I hear Mommy and Daddy fighting about him not working, and about going to Willard's house. Who is Willard, I wonder. Daddy gets mad and comes into the backyard when I am making more cookies. He is mad and says, in a really mean voice, "Get your doll and get in the car, now!" I don't understand what I did. I was only making cookies. Maybe my doll made him mad. I will hold her tight so that he can't hear her if she tries to talk to him. I sit in the truck. I squeeze her. I feel her squeeze me and it feels good to have her arms around me. The little girl is getting scared again. Where is he taking me? I just sit quietly wondering about all the places that we went last in the truck. He pulls into a driveway, but we don't go inside the house; there is a garage in the back and we pull up to it.

Daddy says, "You need to stay in the car, because Willard has pictures of naked women that you shouldn't see." But I want to see. I've never seen these kinds of pictures before. I wonder if they are the same kind of pictures that I see in the magazine Mommy gets. We read picture stories from the magazine and it has words, but I don't know words. Mommy reads the words and stops at a picture and I get to guess what the picture is and that makes a word. I love doing this. I love it when the red magazine comes. I always ask the mailman if he has it today. He laughs at me.

Daddy says, "I'll be right back." I cry because it's hot and I don't want to stay in the truck. He says, "No! Stop the crying. Just be a big girl and sit there. I won't be long" So I freeze again. I stay frozen for a little while, but then I want to see. So I look up and into the garage. There are other people there, some men and some ladies. I have never seen any of them before. I don't see any kids. If I saw kids I would have asked Daddy if I could play with them. I want to see the pictures.

Daddy comes back to the truck after a while. I almost fell asleep while he was gone. He took a long time. He tells me not to tell Mommy because if I do she will be very mad. I don't want to make Mommy mad. Daddy is mad enough and I don't want them to fight. So I just keep that secret, and Daddy says that it will just be our little secret. Secrets don't feel good. But I can do this. I tell the little scared girl inside me the secret though. We talk about it. We are learning what it means to keep secrets.

We go back home and Mommy isn't talking to Daddy. Daddy doesn't tell her where we went. I want to tell her, but I can't. I watch them and I listen to see if Daddy tells her. We all have dinner together and nobody says anything about where we went. I'm tired because I did not get a nap since I went with Daddy. I lie on my couch bed and go to Upside-Down World again and this makes me tired so I fall asleep.

It's morning now and Daddy is already gone. Mommy is looking mad, but Daddy is not here. Mommy says my brother Calvin is coming over and that he just called. She told him not to come over. Mommy is mad that he is not listening to her. Mommy said that he is bringing a woman over and that she is not a good person and that she is called a prostitute. I don't know what a prostitute is. I asked Mommy, but she does not answer me. She pretends I did not say anything.

I ask that little girl and she said she doesn't know either, but she bets it's one of those ladies that has her picture in Willard's garage. The naked pictures that I wasn't allowed to see. Mommy is watching out the front windows for him. We sit on the couch together and Mommy talks and talks. I like to listen to Mommy talk, but it is not happy talk today, so I think I should be scared. But nothing is happening, so maybe I shouldn't. The little girl doesn't know. She said we need to maybe wait and see if anything happens, and that maybe we should be thinking of what we will do if something does. I like it when I plan with the little girl. We plan all the time.

Mommy jumps up and runs to the door. My brother tries to open the door. Mommy stands in front of him. She says, "No, you are not welcome here with that woman. She is not welcome in this home! You don't bring trash like that here." My brother argues with her. I think he might push her like Daddy does. I am sitting on the couch just watching. I am afraid. I hope that man doesn't come again and take me upstairs. That lady just watches too. I wonder if she is thinking how my daddy pushes my Mommy.

The lady is really tanned like she sits in the sun all day. She has very short shorts on. Mommy says something about her shorts, but I can't hear. I want to go closer so that I can hear everything, but I'm too scared. My brother is yelling and looking real mean. He finally leaves the house.

Mommy comes back to the couch and sits by me. She is shaking. She is making the couch move. I don't like it when she shakes because that little girl feels the shaking and feels really, really scared. Mommy picks up that red magazine and starts looking through it. I get excited because I want to play that picture game again. Mommy ignores me when I ask to play the picture game. She doesn't answer me. I think Mommy must have a secret place too or a little girl that she talks to inside her head. I just sit quiet, leaning on Mommy. She puts her arm around me. Mommy covers my legs with a blankie. I fall asleep.

Chapter Twenty

*"You never know how strong you are until being strong
is the only choice you have."*
Cayla Mills

The Exposure

I've started school and I like it a lot. I love to learn things. There is a little boy that keeps kissing me and I don't like that; his name is Brian. I like to play with him, but I don't like him touching me. He won't leave me alone so I try to stay away from him. That is working okay. I've learned to do that a lot since my daddy hurt me. These things just scare me so badly. Now I'm in first grade and another boy keeps bothering me. His name is Patrick. He keeps pinching me on the butt. I am really upset and I don't want to go to school anymore. I wish that he would go away. I tell my teacher and she is so nice. Her name is Mrs. Dennon. She is older than my mommy. It is the end of the school year and Patrick is not in my class anymore and I am so glad. This makes me happy. I can think about my reading now.

I am doing okay in school. I make perfect grades. I never have to study because when I hear something I always remember it. I don't like to read; I have a hard time with that, so I have to remember things. I think I can't read because I'm thinking of all kinds of other stuff. Like I think about what my daddy is doing. I worry about him all day. I think about Mommy too, but she never gets upset, so I think she will be okay. I worry about my sisters, because my daddy is always mean to them and they never do anything. I feel bad for them.

School makes me tired and I have to go to bed early. I awaken again to Daddy and Mommy fighting. I know that they have been drinking for a while. They are both mad at each other. I get up off the couch and this time I don't try to stop them from fighting. Instead, I go to the kitchen and open all the beer. I know Daddy won't drink the beer if they don't have fizz and the fizz goes away if they are opened. If they don't have beer, then they don't fight. It has taken me a long time to figure this all out. I go back to Mommy and Daddy yelling at each other and I tell Daddy what I did. He goes to the kitchen and sees what I have done. I am so scared because I think Daddy is going to get really mad at me now. He comes back and sits down and says nothing. I tell him again what I did and he looks at me and just says, "I know." He had a look on his face that he knew in that moment that I was right. I had done the right thing. We never talked about this either.

I am in fourth grade now and I am in a split classroom. I have bigger kids in my class. They are a grade older. I'm scared. Why do I have to be in a different class? I love to go home for lunch because Mommy always makes me a good lunch. It's raining out and I love to walk in the rain. I love the smell of rain. I have to walk home for lunch.

I have my umbrella and when I am walking I get to the corner and I have to look both ways and wait for any cars. I see a yellow car with a man inside. I stand there waiting for him to turn. He just sits there. He lifts himself up in his seat and I am wondering why he is doing this. He has something in his hand; his privates. I have never seen this before. He is smiling and tries to open the car door. I am so scared. He doesn't look nice. When he looks at me, I feel a warning in the bottom of my stomach. My little girl tells me to run. I run as fast as I can. My little girl is yelling at me to hurry, that I have to beat him to the next corner or he will be able to get me. My legs are hurting. I am breathing hard. The car has circle lights in the back. I remember that. I get to the corner and I know his car will be coming. I run so fast to get across the street. I run in front of his car and he almost hits me. I see a look of desperation on his face. I keep running faster and faster. I get home and Mommy is at the door, watching for me. She asks "Why are you so out of breath?" I tell her what happened. She is frantic. The neighbor, Mrs. Samuels, is there and she says that I am making it up. Mommy argues with her and believes me. I cry and hold on to Mommy. I don't like Mrs. Samuels. She is mean. I am so afraid. Mommy and Mrs. Samuels talk about what that man might have been doing and that he was going to maybe kidnap me. I don't know what kidnap means. I am so scared.

Daddy comes home and Mommy tells him and he is very mad. I have never seen Daddy so mad. He gets in his truck to go and try to find this man. Daddy comes home and could not find him. I am still scared. Daddy takes me back to school and talks to the principal. I tell my teacher, but she doesn't say anything. No one will talk to me about it and I am scared. Is this man going to come to my classroom? Will he be looking for me every day that I walk home from school? Daddy said that he would take me to school for a while because he doesn't want that man to take me. This makes me feel a little better, but I am still scared.

I haven't been bothered on the way to or from school. I'm still worrying. I look for this man every day. There is a boy in my class, but he is in the fifth grade and he keeps following me home from school. He is in my split class, but I am in the fourth grade. He creeps out from behind bushes and buildings and scares me. He doesn't touch me, but he just stops and stares in a creepy way. He laughs and thinks this is funny. I don't! I am scared. His name is Ricky. I tell my sisters and they know his sister. He keeps doing this. It has been a month, and every day he follows me and he looks at me in a funny way and I don't like this. I tell my teacher, Mrs. Roper, and she just looks at me and smiles. I don't know why she would smile. I don't think this is anything funny. I tell my Mommy and she goes to school and talks to the principal. Ricky finally stops bothering me.

I have all these things to worry about: my daddy bothering me, Brian and Patrick bothering me, and now Ricky. Is this ever going to stop? I just am so tired of this. I need to keep that part of my body separate. Bad things keep happening because of that part of my body. I can't remember what I am learning in school. I get all the answers right, but I don't know if I am there or not. It feels like those years haven't happened. This makes me mad because these are my building blocks for the rest of my life and I feel cheated.

My sister Maggie takes all us kids to the movies. I'm so excited. It is going to be fun. Melody, Jody, Maryann, Colin and me. Maggie says that we can have popcorn and candy at intermission if we are nice and get along. Maggie says that we will sit together and she puts me at the end because I am the oldest. I like being the oldest. The movie is funny. It's "The Shaggy Dog." We all laugh at the movie. At intermission, all the girls have to go to the bathroom. Maggie tells Colin and me to stay in our seats. She will take Melody, Jody and Maryann to the bathroom and then come back and take us. Colin and I are getting along very well. I really love Colin. I wish that we didn't fight so much. We are talking about the silly dog and I turn to look and see if Maggie is coming back – and that man is there!

The man in the car on the way home from school for lunch that day. I am frozen. Colin sees that I have stopped talking to him and stopped laughing. I start to cry. He doesn't understand why. I tell him that is the man! That is the same man! He has come to get me. Colin knows about the man because I have told him before. He is worried about me. We look again. The man was just standing at the entrance of the theater. He didn't have any children with him; he was all by himself. Colin holds my hand so that I won't be afraid, but I am still afraid. I am still crying but not so the man can hear. I am crying in my special place again.

Maggie and the girls come back to their seats. Colin tells her I am upset. She comes over and sits by me and asks, "What's the matter?" I tell her and she looks at all us kids and says, "Let's go to the concession stand!" We all get up to go and she holds my hand and keeps me close. I am shaking; I am so scared. She tells the clerk that she needs to speak to the manager. The manager comes over and she takes him aside. We all sit holding hands on the bench in front of the concession stand. We are all worried now. Melody, Jody, and Maryann and Colin are all worried about me. Maggie says we need to sit there for a little while and someone is coming to talk with us.

A policeman comes. It was a different policeman than the one that took my daddy. He sits me on his knee and talks about that man with me. I answer all his questions politely. He asks me if I am really sure. I tell him, "Yes, I will always remember that man. It's the same man!" He goes into the theater and gets the man. He takes him outside and talks with him. We can't hear. The man has to leave. The policeman comes back to us and talks to Maggie and tells her that the man says he has never done anything like that. He was just here to watch the movie. The policeman said that he doesn't have a record. I don't think anyone believes me. I know it was that man. I tell Maggie that no one believes me and she says that she does. Colin, Melody, Jody and Maryann believe me. I tell Mommy and Daddy when I get home. They say that they believe me.

Lilly sat numb. She never would have dreamt that her daughter had felt all this trauma and pain. She was speechless. She quietly sobbed and wondered how she would handle this. How could she help this child to heal? Lilly asked God to help her one last time.

"Please, God, help me to show Sadie a better way; help her to find what I was unable to in my life. Help her to not use my loyalty, determination and dedication, to her despair, the way I have. Help her to move forward and leave this all

behind in a manner that awakens her awareness. Let her pass
this new awakening on to her children and grandchildren.
Please give me the strength to mend things that need
mending. Give to me what I ask, this one last time. Amen."

Lilly reached out to Sadie, and they talked about the diaries. Sadie said that so much of that was behind her, but that she had worked to try and understand it all. She said she had left the diaries there because she didn't want anyone else reading them and felt they would be safe. She was glad that Lilly had found them and not someone else. She was glad that Lilly had read them because it gave them a path for discussion. Sadie treasured the relationship that she had with her mother, the relationship that had come to be. She didn't fault her for not being in the moment; she understood. Lilly could breathe a sigh of relief. She could rest in knowing that Sadie was going to be all right. They hugged and talked daily about the things that Sadie had found so scary growing up. Lilly, with all her wisdom, tried to help Sadie to understand what was happening at the time, and to find a place of acceptance. They both accepted, as nothing could be changed – but much could be understood.

Lilly went to the doctor and received a diagnosis of terminal cancer. It had come back with a vengeance and had spread. There was no chance she would recover. The children were angry because they did not understand how this could happen when all her scans had been good. Later it would come to light that in fact her scans were never good; they had never been taken at all. Lilly had made a conscious choice to say no – I quit – I can't take this anymore. I am tired. I have given all to this house and the walls within it, the people within it. I've done my best – and I'm just tired.

Chapter Twenty-One

*"Life isn't about waiting for the storm to pass…
It's about learning to dance in the rain."*
Vivian Greene

Happy Death

T he children were initially quite upset with Lilly because of her not following through with the cancer treatment as she should. Some saw it as her choice, her right; but others, for selfish reasons, could not. None of them wanted to give their mother up, but some understood her plight and what she had been through. They understood her grief and her sadness and her tiredness, and wanted only for God to hold her now. Lilly suffered one last time at the hands of cancer. She vowed not to leave until after Christmas that year, and that is exactly what she did.

The children all gathered to be with Lilly in her last moments. They had placed a baby monitor in her room so that she would not have to endure any extra effort should she need something. Sadie wanted some alone time with her mother, her last alone time. She had watched for weeks and weeks the suffering that Lilly had gone through, and how everyone had rallied to her care. Sadie had four small children now; she lived out of town and was driving back and forth to be with her mother. She wanted to help her mother. She had witnessed all the suffering and despair that Lilly had been put through, and she respected Lilly for making a difficult choice – but a choice that she had earned.

It was Christmas Day, and Lilly was not doing well. She was, for the most part, in and out of consciousness. She was aware, but to a minimal degree. Sadie entered Lilly's bedroom and sat at her side. She told her mother how much she loved her, and that she wanted her to suffer no more. She told her that she wanted to read her a prayer. Sadie sat and slowly read a prayer for a "Happy Death."

Lord Jesus, by your own sufferings
and sorrow, by your Passion, Death
And life-giving Resurrection, deliver me
from a sudden and un-provided death.
Help me to live always in your grace that
I may always be ready to meet you in joy.
Grant me, Lord, time for repenting of
all my sinfulness. Grant me, Lord,
a happy death in your grace. I ask for salvation
for myself, my family, my friends and relatives,
and for all my brothers and sisters in
Christ. Bring us all safely home to you,
Lord, that we may praise you and bless you forever.
Holy Mary, Mother of God, pray for us sinners,
now and at the hour of our death. Amen.

The Shrine Prayer Book
The Missionary Oblates of Mary Immaculate

Sadie had a special prayer book that she frequently used, and she clutched this. She continued reading as her tears dropped, one after another, onto the page. Lilly held her hand. She found herself sobbing and not wanting to let Lilly go, but at the same time she wanted nothing more for her mother. She hugged her and said her goodbyes. She had finished what she had come to do.

Sadie left Lilly's bedroom and returned to the kitchen where the other family members sat. Everyone was crying. Nobody had turned off the baby monitor, and so everyone had been privy to Sadie's final moments with her mother. Sadie was not offended by this, as she felt comfortable in the way that she had handled her goodbye, and it would not have been any different even if the family had physically been present in the room. The realization had been just a bit unsettling for everyone, yet no one had moved to quiet the monitor.

At 1:15 a.m. on the day following Christmas, Lilly separated her soul from that physical body of pain and despair, and lifted to the beauty beyond. There was no longer a need to be loyal – she had proven her worth in that many times over. Her dedication was reflected in the faces of all the people she loved. There was no need to persevere because she had plowed through cancer three times with a resiliency to be envied. Her dedication was always there, and she had bestowed that upon many a child who had sat upon her lap.

The house still stands that brought all the pain and suffering. The house that gave only brief moments of happiness. Its walls are the same but the people are different. And the people are still suffering within its walls because those walls can talk now: they have stories attached to them, and the forever sadness of a family broken in so many ways, and of one woman who tried so hard to keep them all together, all her babies together, and not adopt them out for others to raise. And she did just that. She raised them all: as dysfunctional as it may have been or may have appeared to others, there was a love and dedication to family that only Lilly was able to deliver.

Sadie has realized that she had spent her life hiding. Hiding from others by being aloof, by putting up walls and not allowing others to get close to her. Mostly she just wanted to hide in shame. She was hiding from the love that she "thought" she would never receive, but longed for, fought for, when she had it everywhere around her. Sadie is a fighter. She is determined and she never gave up. Sadie has always felt alone because she failed to let anyone in. Sadie created the pathways of aloneness, scared-ness, wariness of others, guardedness, anger, and more. She was forced to. She still has many paths to dim or burn out before she can feel whole again. That little girl inside her has suffered, but Sadie is making her surface and realize that that was so far back in time, and that her existence need not be so remote. Sadie is making her well. And before Sadie dies, she wants her to feel complete, as complete as Sadie. Their journey continues as they walk hand in hand through life....

"It has been said, 'time heals all wounds.' I do not agree. The wounds remain. In time, the mind, protecting its sanity, covers them with scar tissue and the pain lessens. But it is never gone."

Rose Kennedy

The Celeste Dupree Cottage

The appealing home pictured on the front of this book is known as the **Celeste Dupree Cottage**. The home came to me while searching for images and I was drawn to it. Once I saw this fascinating home and learned of its richness in the community of Social Circle, no other image would suffice.

Being built in the pre-Civil War era, this home was situated in the heart of downtown Social Circle, Georgia. This lovely home was featured in the article by Karen J. Rohr of the Rockdale Citizen, the local Conyers-Rockdale County, GA newspaper. The home was to be given away free, but the interested parties were required to relocate the home.

At the time, the First Baptist Church of Social Circle owned the historic home and desired it to be moved so that they could expand. They offered $10,000 to assist with the relocation costs; the same amount that would be spent if the home were to be demolished. The church reached an agreement with the Social Circle Historic Preservation Commission to allow one year's time to pass while seeking an interested party for its relocation. The church members wanted to give the home a chance to survive.

According to The Social Circle Historic Preservation Society, the society further attracted potential bidders by agreeing to match the First Baptist Church donation, which increased the acquired moving costs to $20,000. The only stipulation to receiving the funds from the historical society was that the home be moved to a permanent foundation within Social Circle, protected from the elements, until its restoration. It was estimated at the time, that the cost of moving the home, would be approximately $50,000.

The home, built in the late 1850's, is a one story Victorian cottage displaying three fireplaces, hardwood floors, several bedrooms, living room, dining area, two bathrooms and a large foyer. This home belonged to Celeste Sigman Dupree, a successful business woman, and historic preservation advocate. She had grown up in the home and her parents had remained there throughout their lives. She was passionate about the old homes of Social Circle and concerned for their wellbeing. After her death in 2005, the First Baptist Church purchased the property and her home in 2007.

The home also appeared in an article of *"This Old House Magazine"* by Paul Hope, featuring its needs, amenities, and why it should be saved. Social Circle resident, Michael Owens, decided to save the lovely cottage and underwent the monumental task of having the home moved. It now sits on a property adjacent to a Greek Revival Mansion known as Magnolia Manor, which itself has a very rich heritage. Magnolia Manor is a catering and special events facility. Mr. Owens plans to renovate the Dupree Cottage to expand the current Magnolia Manor.

Mr. Tom Brown, photographer, and Mr. Michael Owens, homeowner, both of Social Circle, Georgia, have graciously allowed me the use of this image for my book. Donations towards the renovation of this beautiful Greek Revival pre-Civil War home can be sent to Mike Owens, Celeste Dupree Home Restoration, P.O. Box 91, Social Circle, GA 30025.

References:
Karen J. Rohr, "Church Seeks Takers to Relocate Historic Social Circle Home," Rockdale Citizen, Conyers-Rockdale County, GA, December 8, 2012.

Paul Hope, "Save This Old House," *This Old House Magazine*, May 2013, http://www.thisoldhouse.com/toh/magazines

Photograph by Tom Brown

About the Author

Photo by HD Photography Atlanta

Cheryle Boyle has had a life-long love of writing from a very early age. She has seized the opportunity to pursue her dream of writing professionally. She has many notebooks full of her works from over the years, and now that the time has come, she looks forward to sharing these with her readers.

While her journey as a professional author is new, with her past employment as a legal assistant to a state senator, medical, legal and psychiatric transcriptionist, as well as, psychological assistant, she offers in depth insight into the workings of the human spirit. Her experience is brilliantly reflected in her writing.

She has lived in several states while relocating for her husband's job, i.e., Kansas, Illinois, New Jersey, Michigan, California and Georgia. While each state offers a different point of view about life, Cheryle remains steadfast in her belief that location is not relative, as long as family is close by.

Cheryle is a wife, mother of four and grandmother to 12. She enjoys spending time with her family and making memories, as well as sewing, quilting, intricate French heirloom sewing, cooking, decorating and anything creative. For more details, please visit Cheryle's website at www.CheryleBoyle.com